IN THE HOT SEAT

"Brandon probably doesn't feel comfortable telling all of us his deepest secrets without getting something in return. Right, Brandon?"

"Right, whatever you say." Brandon had no idea where Andrea was headed, but at the moment she was his only ally.

"I think we should all tell one of our fantasies, something we've always dreamed about. That way, it's more like a game instead of an inquisition." It seemed like a reasonable compromise to Brandon and he smiled at her gratefully. Sometimes Andrea Zuckerman just seemed to know exactly how he felt.

"Yeah, let's make it a game of 'what if'?" Brenda sat up straight, excited. "What if we had the perfect life, what would a typical day be like? This is so hot!"

Don't miss these books in the exciting
BEVERLY HILLS, 90210 series

Beverly Hills, 90210

Beverly Hills, 90210—Exposed!

Beverly Hills, 90210—No Secrets

Beverly Hills, 90210—Which Way to the Beach?

And, coming soon

Beverly Hills, 90210—'Tis the Season

Published by
HARPERPAPERBACKS

SPELLING ENT. INC.

FANTASIES

A novel by
K.T. Smith

Based on the television series created by
Darren Star

HarperPaperbacks
A Division of HarperCollins*Publishers*

HarperPaperbacks   *A Division of* HarperCollins*Publishers*
                     10 East 53rd Street, New York, N.Y. 10022

Front and back cover photos by Timothy White
Insert photos by Timothy White and Andrew Semel

First printing: August 1992

Printed in the United States of America

HarperPaperbacks and colophon are trademarks of HarperCollins*Publishers*

❖ 10 9 8 7 6 5 4 3 2 1

Prologue

"IT'S OVER," BRENDA WALSH ANNOUNCED AS she turned toward Dylan McKay. Kelly Taylor and Donna Martin stared at each other speechless as the fire crackled loudly in the silence. Glancing at her two friends' confused faces, Brenda giggled. "The summer, you guys! The summer! I mean, it's basically over. After this weekend it's back to alarm clocks and cracking the books." Brenda grimaced at the thought of it all. "I don't even have anything new to wear." She pouted and lifted her face expectantly toward Dylan. Chuckling, he tousled Brenda's long chestnut hair as he smiled down at her.

"Yeah, Bren, it's just a matter of time now before our lives are run by the sound of the bell again." He squeezed her tightly and looked out at the ocean. "It's really been a great summer, though, hasn't it?" His raspy voice was wistful.

Kelly turned to Steve Sanders and rolled her eyes, knowing Dylan would start listing all the reasons why life was so wonderful. They all knew where his monologue would eventually end up—surfing and Brenda. Since Brenda and Dylan had gotten back together, that's all he seemed to care about. Everyone had heard it before, and with a bit of luck they wouldn't have to suffer through it again. She eyed Steve and silently pleaded with him to do something before it was too late. He shrugged in mock exasperation then turned away.

"The surf was awesome, the Green Room was kicking, the nights were definitely—" Dylan's voice was muffled as Brenda covered his mouth with her hand.

"Dylan, you promised you wouldn't kiss and tell!" She laughed and tried to squirm away as he grabbed her arms and pulled her back toward him.

Brandon Walsh threw a piece of wood on the fire with a hollow thud, trying to hold back the cool evening breeze that was blowing off of the water. As he brushed his hands off on his jeans, he turned to Dylan and shook his head. "I guess if you call busting your butt every day at the beach club a good time, D., yeah, it's been great—magnificent even!"

Dylan looked up at Brandon warily. Over the past year they had become pretty tight and Dylan could tell something was definitely eating at his friend. "What gives, Walsh?"

"Well, it's like this, Hobson." Brandon ran his fingers abruptly through his hair and eyed Dylan squarely. "Every single morning I drag myself out of bed at the crack of dawn, throw my clothes on, catch a six-thirty bus, and head on down to the Beach Club. For what?"

Steve snorted loudly as Brandon warmed to his topic. This was *definitely* not what he had in mind when he talked David Silver and Donna into getting everyone together for a "sayonara summer" party. A little music, some beach blankets, a blazing fire, and the summer stars all added up to what could have been a great way to end summer vacation. But no, the "B" man was on a roll and now all everyone could do was sit back and wait for him to lose steam.

"Sure, I wanted to work this summer, I admit that. But I can think of several hundred, maybe even a thousand, quite possibly a million other things I'd rather do with my time than pick up dirty beach towels all day long. You wanna talk about slave work! You know what I mean?" Brandon looked around the fire, searching for some sign of sympathy.

When he caught her eye, Kelly couldn't hold back and collapsed laughing on the blanket. Brandon's cheeks flushed and he stared hard at her as she tried to regain her composure.

"How would you like it, Kelly, if you were at someone's beck and call every minute of the day? Let me tell you, it's definitely not what I'd call a good time. It got so bad that after a while I had to keep checking my name tag, I really started to think my name was Sonny."

Kelly's giggles grew contagious and soon Brandon was surrounded by stifled laughter as his friends tried to hide their amusement. Donna grinned at him sweetly as if she actually understood how he felt, then slowly rubbed her two index fingers and thumbs together in unison.

"Just what's that supposed to mean?" Brandon asked, indignant.

"The smallest violins in the world in stereo." She smirked at him openly as Brandon's hands shot out, grabbing for her. But Donna pulled back just as Brandon lost his balance and fell forward. His cries of protest were squelched as his face was buried in the sand. Lying there helpless, he could feel marshmallows and popcorn bouncing off his back as Brenda and Kelly mimicked his complaints.

"All right, all right," he said as he pushed himself up from the sand, brushing his face clean. "I get the hint, no need to rub it in."

Brenda watched her twin with an amused gleam in her eye. Since they had moved from Minneapolis, it seemed like Brandon could get so preachy sometimes, and that was definitely not cool in Beverly Hills. It was good for him to get grilled once in a while.

Brandon glared at her. "Very funny, huh, Bren? With a sister like you, a guy would be better off with enemies."

"Brandon, that's really not fair. If you want to play the game, you've got to pay the price." Kelly and Donna nodded in agreement.

Bewildered, Brandon looked over to Andrea for support. "Who's playing a game? All I did was say—"

"We know what you said, Walsh, and we definitely don't want to hear it again." Dylan cocked his head at his friend then continued. "You had to have some fun this summer surrounded by all those tan bathing beauties."

"Yeah, but those tan beauties all had their eyes on the guys on the beach, not the ones in uniform," Steve commented, knowing this was a major sore spot with Brandon.

"You know, you guys, I used to like you—" Brandon said, but Brenda interrupted before things could grow more heated.

"Okay, Brandon, so this summer wasn't the way you thought it would be. Fine. Life goes on. If it was that bad, you don't have to keep talking about it, it's over."

"Besides it's not like you were in prison or something. Nobody forced you to take the job at the Beach Club," Donna added, trying to follow Brenda's lead.

Brandon scowled, knowing he was outnumbered. How could kids with platinum credit cards, cellular phones, and Beemers understand where he was coming from? He hung his head dejectedly as Andrea Zuckerman patted his knee.

"Anyway, if you had a choice, what would you have liked to do this summer?" David Silver asked. Everyone looked at him quizzically as if he had spoken in French. He had been so quiet they had almost forgotten he was there. "What I mean is, what else could you have done this summer? You needed a job and you wanted to be at the beach. It seems to me the job at the Beach Club was the perfect solution."

Brandon shrugged and gazed unhappily into the fire. "I guess you're right, Silver. It's just that I wish something exciting could have happened. I'm young, I'm available, I'm ready." Brandon ignored Dylan's wolf whistle. "Every single day just seemed to run into the next. Sun, sand, and string bikinis that had no interest in a guy like me wearing a green polo shirt." He pulled his knees up to his chest and rested his arms loosely on top.

"Poor, neglected Brandon," Kelly taunted from across the darting flames.

Brenda laughed with her friend then pushed Brandon's shoulder lightly. "Yeah, really. Snap out of it, will you? We're supposed to be having a good time here." Brandon said nothing and kept peering into the flames.

"Okay, say you had a wish, right?" She leaned toward him as Brandon raised his eyes suspiciously. "If you could have one wish to do whatever you wanted with your life, what would you do? What would be your ultimate fantasy?"

His face burned a deep crimson as hoots of laughter and catcalls erupted from the guys. Sometimes his sister could be so dense. He shot Steve and Dylan deadly looks, silencing their boisterous remarks. "Bren, I really don't think this has anything to do with—"

"I don't mean romantic or sexual fantasies, Brandon. You guys are so predictable! I swear, you only have your minds on one thing!" She deftly moved her head as Dylan whispered in her ear playfully and tried to push him away. "For those of you who can't seem to understand," she said, looking pointedly at Steve and David, "what I'm talking about is what would be the coolest thing you could see yourself doing, say in ten years?"

Brandon shifted uncomfortably on the blanket.

"Come on, Brandon, you have to have some fantasies," Kelly needled him. "Don't you ever just let yourself go and daydream?"

"Sure he does, but I don't think you could handle his fantasies, Kelly." Steve chuckled loudly, then tried to keep a straight face when she glared at him and threw a handful of sand his way. He ducked expectantly, but the sand fell short, landing in the fire and temporarily dousing the flames.

"Everyone has fantasies, Steve, and they don't always have to be X-rated." Andrea raised her voice above the sounds of sizzling coals. "It's just not that easy to tell them to other people. Brandon probably doesn't feel comfortable telling all of us his deepest secrets without getting something in return. Right, Brandon?"

"Yeah, right, whatever you say." Brandon had no idea where Andrea was headed, but at the moment she was his only ally.

"I think we should all tell one of our fantasies, something we've always dreamed about. That way, it's more like a game instead of an inquisition." It seemed like a reasonable compromise to Brandon and he smiled at her gratefully. Sometimes Andrea Zuckerman just seemed to know exactly how he felt.

"Yeah, let's make it a game of 'what if'?" Brenda sat up straight, excited. "What if we had the perfect life, what would a typical day be like? This is so hot!" She nodded enthusiastically at Kelly and Donna.

"Wait, wait, stop. I think we should lay some ground rules here, Brenda," Kelly said in a serious tone. "Otherwise, some of us could get totally out of control. Each person should get to tell their fantasy without any comments from anyone else. Right, Steve?" she said pointedly as he raised his hands to his chest in disbelief. "That means you and David and Dylan—"

"Whoa, whoa, whoa—wait a minute! What about you and Donna? The sarcasm twins? It think us guys need some protection, too," Dylan said as Brandon voiced his agreement.

"All right, okay, enough!" Andrea interrupted them. "Here's the rules. No one can interrupt or make any comments while someone else is telling their fantasy. If you have something to say, save it until the end. We'll go all the way around the circle counterclockwise. Brandon, you start." Steve still looked skeptical, as if he didn't quite follow her. She sighed heavily, then explained: "Brandon goes first, then Brenda, Dylan, Kelly—Steve, you're fourth—Donna next, then David, and I go last."

"Hey, what a minute!" Steve protested. "How come you get to go last?"

Andrea smiled at him sweetly and said, "Because, Steve, I'm the one that thought of it."

"Well, I don't know if I want to do it. I've never even thought about life after West Beverly. I don't even think about life after next weekend! What am I supposed to say when it gets to be my turn?"

"I'm sure that with your imagination, Steve, by the time we get to you, you'll have thought of something. You always do." Kelly and Donna snickered as Andrea coolly turned her attention back to Brandon. Steve hunched over, his brow creased with effort as he racked his brain.

A dry piece of wood suddenly burst in the flames with a loud pop, sending showers of sparks onto the blankets. As the fire grew stronger everyone watched Brandon expectantly. The silence was broken only by the sounds of the surf in the distance.

Brandon swallowed nervously and cleared his throat. "So I guess it's my turn, huh?" Seven pairs of eyes stared back at him. "You sure you want to do this? Couldn't we play Trivial Pursuit or how about charades, that's always good for some laughs, hey? Hobson, what do you say?"

"Brandon." Brenda's voice carried a warning signal and he knew that if he didn't start soon, his sister would make his life even more miserable than it was right now. Him and his big mouth! He knew he never should have said anything about his summer. *Too late now, Walsh.* I sure wish I was back in Minnesota, Brandon thought as he took a deep breath. They never played stupid games like this back there. There was no way out and he knew it was better to get it over with quickly. He coughed and cleared his throat.

"Well, after high school, I headed east to . . ."

The cool night air descended and everyone moved in closer to the warmth of the fire, listening intently as Brandon spoke.

Brandon

THE SIX-SEATER PROP PLANE CIRCLED SLOWLY, flying just above the barren treetops. Curious, Brandon Walsh peeked out the side window then quickly jerked his head back. "You sure this guy can fly?" he whispered hoarsely.

Dave Samuels, a veteran cameraman for the network, laughed openly at Brandon's uneasiness. "Listen, kid, this is a pleasure cruise compared to some of the press flights I've been on." Brandon wasn't reassured and closed his eyes tightly to prevent his anxiety from showing. This was definitely not what he expected when he agreed to take on this assignment. The bureau chief in Rome, Paul Cale, had made it sound like a piece of cake when he called Brandon into his cluttered, cramped office.

"Okay, Walsh, you were just telling me the other

day you needed a challenge. Here you go." A file bursting with papers skid across the battered desk. Brandon
grabbed at it just as it slid off the edge. "The fighting
has stepped up in western Creatia. It looks like the
rebels are going to storm the capital within seventy-two
hours. Things are ready to explode and we need someone there. You up for it?"

Brandon's eyes glittered with excitement. He had
been waiting for an opportunity like this ever since the
day he picked up his degree from Columbia. "You bet
I'm up for it, just point the way and I'm outta here!" He
stopped short and looked at his boss cautiously, aware
of the unspoken tension between them. Since his
assignment to the Rome office, Brandon always
seemed to be on the outs with Paul. He knew Paul felt
he was too ambitious for his own good, but Brandon
wanted his fifteen minutes of fame and was ready to
fight for it no matter what it cost him. "So what's the
catch, Cale?" he asked, trying to keep his tone light.

"No catch, Walsh, it's strictly business. I'm sending
Dave Samuels out with you. We'll need some really killer
footage. Skeeter Brown's getting his plane prepped now.
With those two crazies, I figure even a greenhorn like
you should be able to stay out of trouble."

Brandon burned at the offhand insult. He knew he
wasn't as experienced as the other correspondents at
the bureau, but he hated being treated like a kid. Even
so, he knew silence was the smartest reaction to his
boss's comment.

"You should get in and get out within forty-eight
hours. Skeeter will drop you off at a temporary landing
field just outside the capital. Since martial law has been
in effect for several weeks, you should be prepared for
the worst. Don't expect a welcome wagon, Walsh.
Americans are not the most popular people in Eastern
Europe these days. Take the file with you and read
through it. There's enough information there to give

you a solid background on the conflict, which you can use as a foundation for your piece."

Brandon flipped through the papers quickly, then looked up. "Can I ask why you're letting me cover this instead of Williams?" Jeff Williams was one of the best correspondents in the business working out of Rome. Brandon knew he wouldn't willingly pass up a high-profile assignment like this. Paul cleared his throat guiltily, as if he had been caught with his hand in the till.

"Well, Walsh, it seems that good old Jeff got himself in a bit of a tight spot last evening over a lovely lady by the name of Lucita at a local pub. Never realized that Lucita's husband happened to be the bartender. Jeff is now an unexpected guest at St. Joseph's Hospital, where he is recovering from his numerous cuts, bruises, and a broken nose, to say nothing about his shattered ego. Looks like he'll be there for at least two days." Paul shook his head.

Even though Brandon felt sorry for Jeff, whose work he admired, he couldn't contain his excitement at this stroke of good fortune. "Yes!" he shouted, and slapped his hand against Paul's desk.

His spirited outburst was cut short when Paul said dryly, "I wouldn't look at this assignment too lightly, Walsh. The body count keeps rising over there and I hate to be the one to tell you, bullets don't care who their victims are. Be careful." Paul gathered up some reports and started for the door. Brandon kept his eyes averted, not sure what to do. "You've got forty-eight hours and that's it. In and out. And remember, don't push it, Walsh." The door slammed after him and Brandon stood still, his back to the door. Then a wide grin broke out on his face, and his cheeks grew flushed. *Welcome to the big time, Brandon baby!* If only the guys from West Beverly could see him now. He silently thanked the gods for looking after him and turned to find his cameraman in the newsroom.

The noises of the bureau offices soothed Brandon's jitters. Voices calling, phones ringing, computers spitting out the latest wire stories through printers, it all seemed comfortably familiar to him now. It had taken six years of gofer jobs and long hours at the network, but here it was, his big chance.

"Anyone seen Samuels?" Brandon yelled over the newsroom din. A distant voice pointed him in the direction of the coffee room, where he found the cameraman hunched over a steaming cup of coffee.

Dave Samuels had been around the circuit for years and his face bore numerous battle scars. In his late forties, Samuels preferred to keep his graying curly hair long, even though it was a hassle to deal with when he was on assignment and not sure when he might take his next shower. Deep brown, bloodshot eyes perched above his heavily bearded cheeks, completing the illusion of a world-weary rebel. When Brandon zoomed into the room, Samuels glanced up briefly then closed his eyes and continued to hold his face over the thin wisps of steam drifting up from his cup.

"Hey, Samuels, isn't it great, man? You and me, bud, heading out to the big-W zone for some major footage—yes!" Brandon dragged a chair across the floor and sat down.

"Dandy, it's just dandy," Samuels answered sarcastically as he kept his eyes tightly closed.

Brandon was undaunted. "I think I'll head back to my apartment and grab some things. How long before you think Skeeter will be ready to head out?" He cracked his knuckles and leaned forward in his chair.

Samuels shook his head wearily, rubbing his hand roughly through his beard. "As soon as you get there, lover boy, I imagine." Despite his resentment of Cale for being put up as a watchdog over a novice in the field, Samuels found himself warming to the younger man's enthusiasm. Sometimes he didn't know why he just didn't take early retirement. These assignments always added a few more gray hairs to his already ample thatch. With a silent curse at the bureau chief, he pulled himself up from the table. "I got the gear together already, so I think I'll just head on over to the airport and see if I can't lend old Skeeter a hand or something. You just come over when you're ready. Okay, hotshot?" He grabbed his coffee then looked Brandon directly in the eye. "You know, you really should think twice about this assignment, Walsh. It's not a game."

Brandon fumed as he watched the cameraman walk out, wondering what was eating at him. Maybe Dave had a run-in with Lucita's husband, too. He grinned and shook his head. Determined not to let anyone ruin his good time, he jumped up and grabbed his tattered black leather jacket from the back of the chair. Whistling an old R.E.M. tune casually to himself, he strode across the crowded newsroom to the elevators, oblivious to the curious stares from several of the other staff members. He was on his way to the big time now, it was just a matter of time, he could feel it. As the elevator doors slid open Brandon jumped in eagerly without looking back.

Skeeter Brown twisted around in the yellowed vinyl pilot's seat. "We should be landin' in a few minutes. This old lady needs to rest a bit," he said affectionately as he patted the worn control board.

Brandon smiled wanly, his initial excitement lost after the long, bumpy flight. "Where are you going to land this thing?" he asked hoarsely. The one thing Brandon wanted right now more than anything was some nice firm land he could squeeze between his toes.

Dave chuckled as he listened expectantly for

Skeeter's response. "Well, the airport was demolished by some SAM bombardments a few weeks back. Airports are always one of the first targets in fightin' like this. So I been landing wherever I see about a hundred feet of clear, flat land," Skeeter explained. Brandon's face paled as he realized what he was in for and braced himself for the sudden descent. If he had learned anything on the short flight from Rome, it was to expect the worst. So much for the glamour of bright lights!

As the plane lost altitude quickly he raised his eyes to the sky and pleaded for mercy. With a sudden dip and several bounces, they somehow managed to slide to a stop just a few feet from an old, dilapidated wooden barn.

"Yee-haw! That one sure was a beauty! They just don't make gals like this one anymore." Skeeter slipped smoothly out of his seat and onto the ground, then reached over to open the side door. With more energy than he thought he had left in his body, Brandon grabbed his bag and climbed down. The sounds of rustling luggage reminded him that Dave had several heavy bags of gear to carry. Reluctantly, he reached up and pulled two black cases down then waited for his partner to join him.

The field was more mud than anything. Lines of hardening tracks told the tale of many landings like the one Brandon had just experienced. A narrow, pitted dirt trail led from the barn out to the main road, which winded through the hillside west toward the city. Brandon could see dark puffs of smoke off in the distance. His heartbeat picked up a pace as he looked out over the war-scarred countryside. This was it, no turning back now.

"Pretty eerie, isn't it?" Brandon hadn't heard Dave come up beside him.

"I've never seen action this close before," Brandon

said, not wanting to admit the fear he felt building inside his gut.

Dave looked out at the horizon, then turned to him and said, "The first few times are really tough. Then you get so hardened, it doesn't matter if there's a missile on your tail—there's a story to be had and you're the one who's here to get it."

Brandon was surprised at the older man's intuition. He started to say how much he appreciated Dave's understanding when the cameraman spoke again. "Besides, you're too much of a pain in the butt to get shot at. Come on, enough sight-seeing. We got a job to do." With a grunt, he lifted up several of the bags and set off toward the barn where an old gray Jeep sat waiting.

"Now, y'all remember, I'll be back in forty-eight hours. Keep an eye out for me and the old lady here. If you guys aren't here when I show up, you're on your own, got it?" Skeeter agilely climbed back into the plane, not waiting to hear an answer. With a quick wave he called out, "Y'all enjoy your vacation now, y'hear?" and started the props. As the plane rolled away Brandon mumbled to himself, wondering again just what he had gotten himself into.

The drive into the city was difficult. The roadway had been targeted by missiles the night before and downed power lines lay exposed on the cracked pavement. The driver, a local man cashing in on the sudden influx of newspeople, made his way cautiously through the debris. As they passed each sizzling piece of cable Brandon felt his wavy brown hair stand up straight, as if electrified by the acrid air.

Finally the Jeep reached the battered remains of the city center. Half-standing buildings surrounded a small square where abandoned cars lay ruined.

Brandon leaned forward. "So where is there to stay around here?" he asked. The driver looked at him skeptically, then broke into a fit of laughter.

"What's so funny?" Brandon asked indignantly. He gripped the edge of the front seat.

"I think he's laughing because that was the dumbest question he's heard in a long time," Dave said dryly. "Take a hard look around you, Walsh. Do you see any tourism signs? Anything saying 'Welcome to Creatia, Vacationland of Eastern Europe'?" He shook his head in amazement as he opened the car door and got out.

The driver's snickers continued as he unloaded their bags onto the sidewalk. As he drove away, his dry laughter was carried back through the open car windows.

Stung by the ridicule, Brandon stalked off toward an undamaged building across the square, determined to find a place to stay.

"Now don't go and get your nose out of joint, Brandon," Dave called out to him from across the street. Brandon turned, then waited as the cameraman scuttled over, burdened by his heavy load.

"There's a small hostel around the corner that I heard some crews are using as a base of operations. We'll head over there and see what's on the board, maybe find us some space to squeeze into." Dave walked past and Brandon followed him reluctantly, not wanting to admit just how much he had to learn about life on assignment.

The hostel was an old three-story brick tenement building, brimming with crews from every network. Brandon called out to a few familiar faces as he made his way cautiously through the huge open marble lobby. Temporary workstations made of plastic crates and black cases had sprouted up wherever space allowed and the entire tile floor was covered by a huge tangle of computer cables. With a keen eye, Brandon scoured the room, looking for a small space they could claim.

"Excuse me, but you seem to be standing on my cables."

Brandon swung around, startled.

"Are you deaf? I said you're standing on my cables!" The young woman's icy green eyes flashed with impatience as she bent down to push at his immobile legs. Brandon chuckled and held his feet firm. "I am really getting rather annoyed with you," she said, looking up at him.

"Forgot about me already, Marissa?" Brandon held her stare as he reached down and gently pulled her chin up, closing her open mouth. "I mean, it's only been six years since Columbia, I couldn't have changed that much." He held his hand out and helped her to her feet.

"Brandon, I can't believe it!" Marissa Vincente threw her arms around his neck and held him tightly. "I can't believe it's really you. What are you doing here?"

"I've been working for CSN out of Rome for the past year and I finally got a good break. Just here to cover the next forty-eight hours and then back to the home plate, I guess. What about you? What have you been doing since you got back to Italy?"

Brandon had known back in college that Marissa had major talent. The kind you spelled with a capital *T*. That was part of the problem between them. So many times he had felt like he was in competition with her instead of just being in love with her. Eventually it had gotten so intense that they'd had to go their separate ways. It had been a painful break and Brandon knew that Marissa had taken more than a small piece of him with her when she left New York. He couldn't believe that he would run into her here, of all places. He smiled tenderly as he watched her brush away the cas-

cade of dark curls falling across her face. A distant
memory teased at his mind, Marissa's tawny skin glowing in the darkness. Brandon shifted uncomfortably
and folded his arms across his chest.

"Well, after graduation I took the summer off and
did a Europass tour. When September rolled around,
my father managed to get me an interview for a floor
director at ITN." She laughed lightly at his expression.
"I know, I know. I always said it was beneath me! But
when it's the only thing available, you just have to do
what you have to do. It was an in and I took it. After
about six months of pointing at cameras and cueing
the on-air talent, I filled in for a reporter and voilà!
Here I am." She held her arms out wide and smiled
matter-of-factly at Brandon.

"Italian Television Network, huh? Not bad, Maris,
not bad." He had always known she would end up on
her feet, that was one of the reasons he had fallen for
her. That and her drop-dead gorgeous body that
seemed to have grown even sleeker in the past six
years. Brandon ran his eyes appreciatively down her
long legs then back up to her face. "It's really great to
see you," he said huskily. Her eyes bore into him and
Brandon felt himself being drawn toward her.

"So, I see you two stars have already met." Dave
Samuels appeared at Brandon's side. Marissa leaned
over and kissed him lightly on the cheek. "How are
you, Davida?" she asked.

"Other than a few rough spots here and there, as
smooth as ever, kiddo. How about you?" Brandon felt a
unexpected pang of jealousy at their easy familiarity.
As if he could sense it, Dave turned to him and
explained, "Marissa and I have been in one or two hot
spots together over the past few years. I've known her
since she was just a gofer." Marissa chuckled.

"Yeah, Marissa and I go way back, too, don't we?"
Brandon looked at her expectantly, but she just smiled.

"So where's the action at, M.V.?" With the clock ticking against them, Dave was anxious to get moving on their piece.

"Actually I was just finishing up some notes here then I was going to go toward the capital building. I have a pickup truck if you want to come along. My camera crew went down this morning to get early footage, so there's plenty of room." She grinned suggestively at Brandon.

"Where can we dump some of this gear?" he asked.

"The upstairs rooms are all taken by the long-timers. Your best bet is to grab some floor space here in the lobby and make camp. That's what we did." She gestured toward her makeshift desk, surrounded by mounds of camera gear. Dave readily agreed and soon they had managed to claim a small area behind a thick plaster pillar and created a workable space.

"Marissa, how long have you been assigned here?" Brandon asked as Dave stood back, admiring their work. Marissa's cool confidence in the face of danger blew him away.

"Only two days. It's been hectic, but I think things are just starting to get tense. The rebels are coming in from the west, making their way toward the capital. If all goes as planned, we ought to see some heavy fighting sometime tonight." Excitement glowed in her face as she talked, her cheeks flushed against the almost black mass of curls sprouting from her head. Brandon caught himself and pulled back, remembering his priorities.

"Hey, Dave, my man, we need to get our butts down to the capital area and get some good bites before too long. Then I'll come back and do a foundation so we can have something to transmit tonight." Brandon glanced around the lobby then turned back to Marissa. "Do you have some type of updated report on the situation I could look over? I need to get my bearings on where this story should go."

A flicker of admiration passed through her eyes as she reached over and handed him a full-page report. "Hot off the press," she said jokingly. As Brandon breezed through it he could feel her watching him and knew that this was going to be one of the biggest challenges of his life—both professionally and personally. His heart did a small two-step as he continued reading, trying to focus his brain on the spot they were heading out to shoot.

"The fighting continues as the rebel forces have made their way to within blocks of the capital building. Sources say that the next six hours are critical." A long shrill whistle followed by a nearby explosion drowned out Brandon's words, but he continued. "If the government of Creatia is to survive this latest onslaught, the time is now for them to take a hard-line stand. I'm Brandon Walsh for CSN News in Bukarah, Creatia."

Suddenly the street behind Brandon exploded, sending chunks of concrete high into the air. He dived headfirst to the ground, holding his hands protectively over his head as debris from the bombing rained down around him. A thick, chilling silence followed.

"Way to go, Brandon! Yes!" Dave applauded loudly from behind a battered truck as Brandon pushed himself up off the ground. Crewmen from other networks working close by filtered over to their area and joined in until Brandon was surrounded by a small audience.

"Are you guys crazy? I could have been killed just now!" Brandon stared at his cameraman accusingly.

"But you weren't and I've never, in all my years behind the camera, seen a better close than that. Talk about punctuation and special effects! Let's see what they say about this piece back in New York." Dave swung around and talked excitedly to the people around him as Brandon took a deep breath and tried to regain his composure. Sirens blared across the city as the flash bombings continued. Oblivious to the danger, Dave rewound the videotape and called for Brandon to join the small group behind the monitor. Reluctantly he watched, and had to admit it was excellent footage. With bombed-out buildings in the background and the unexpected explosion at the close, Brandon knew it was extremely effective reporting. He shook hands warmly with some of the newspeople who congratulated him. Fame was fleeting in this business, so he didn't think too hard on his apparent success. The piece could be buried by one of those heart-wrenching human-interest stories. He smirked as he leaned back against the tailgate of the pickup.

The abrupt sounds of close gunfire dampened his exhilaration and he hastily gathered up his notes then grabbed his leather jacket and started to head back to the hostel. Dave was immersed in editing the tape to send by satellite to the network, so Brandon had some downtime to sit back and recuperate from his close call. Yes, sir, this was definitely what he had been waiting for, Brandon thought as he waved good-bye to Dave and hitched a ride with a passing news van.

The lobby was nearly empty. Brandon made his way through the tangled maze of discarded belongings and collapsed onto the small pile of bags they had left behind. His body was tense, racing with adrenaline. This was just too cool! Here he was smack in the middle of a major story. As he stared up at the ornate plaster ceiling, his mind wandered back to the days when he worked as a reporter on the *Beverly Blaze*—Andrea would have killed to be on a story this hot! As exhaustion overtook him Brandon's eyes grew heavy and he sank deeper into his makeshift bed. Soon his steady breathing echoed throughout the lobby, interrupted only by the sounds of the wire stories being spit out of a nearby printer.

The sound of a popping cork jerked him awake sometime later. As he wiped at his sleep-strained eyes, he saw the entire lobby was filled with people. Each one seemed to be holding a glass, raised in some kind of mock-military salute.

"What the heck is . . ." Brandon frowned as he tried to sit up. Dave pushed his way through the crowd and came forward with a dusty champagne bottle in his right hand, two dirty glasses in his left.

"Well, superstar, we thought we'd have ourselves a little celebration, now that your pretty face is known throughout the entire world." The glint in his eye spelled trouble and Brandon knew he was in for it. As if on cue, several of the guys started chanting, and soon Brandon was surrounded by the sounds of "superstar" bouncing off the marble walls of the lobby.

"What are you talking about, Samuels?" Brandon was completely confused and a bit irritated. Talk about rude awakenings!

"Well, Brandon, it seems that when your piece aired tonight, the network switchboard lit up with calls from thousands of concerned females across the country. They all wanted to be assured that your gorgeous hide was still in one piece." Dave put out his hand and pulled Brandon to his feet. As he poured the champagne someone started the chant again. Brandon's face turned beet red.

"Silence, please," Dave yelled. "A toast to the man of the hour, Brandon Walsh, who from this day forward shall be known to one and all as the Superstar." Cheers and laughter echoed through the room as Brandon sipped his champagne good-naturedly. The party seemed to gather speed as old friends greeted new ones and the fighting was momentarily forgotten.

"So how does it feel to be a superstar?" Marissa

appeared out of nowhere, her voice tinged with laughter.

"It doesn't feel like anything. I was sound asleep when Dave started this. I still haven't absorbed it all yet."

"I know." Marissa smiled secretively. "I'm the one that found you. Everyone was searching outside, but I had a feeling that you'd be in here." She inched a bit closer. "Care to offer the lady a taste of your champagne?"

The invitation in her smile made Brandon nervous. It wasn't as if he didn't know Marissa; that was the problem. She was dangerous and he knew it, but he couldn't make himself walk away again. He steadied his hand as he offered his glass to her, trying to be casual. "Come on, Maris, I'm sure this type of thing happens around here all the time, right?"

"Not since I've been here." She sipped the champagne and twitched her nose at him. "Tickles." As she swallowed slowly, Brandon noticed a small drop on the tip of her nose and reached out to brush it off. The warmth of her skin held him and she raised her face toward him.

"So what are you two gorgeous people doing hiding back here?" Dave placed an arm around each of their shoulders, moving them forward as he spoke. Brandon smiled at him affectionately.

"You know your timing is pretty off, Samuels," he said jokingly as he slipped away. Dave started to protest then gave up as Brandon quickly pulled Marissa with him into a small alcove.

"That wasn't very friendly of you," she said as she leaned against the wall.

"I wasn't trying to be friendly," he answered flippantly. He reached for the empty glass. Suddenly Marissa wrapped her arms around his neck. Uncertain, Brandon looked into her eyes. Something passed between them and she parted her lips invitingly. Brandon kissed her softly, then more passionately. He ran his fingers through her hair, feeling the silky curls slip away.

"Brandon, I know that when we split up, I didn't really give you much of a chance—"

The explosion rocked the walls of the hostel. Complete darkness surrounded them as screams erupted everywhere and plaster poured down from the ceiling. The marble columns seemed to teeter and then fell thunderously to the floor. Brandon grabbed for Marissa's hand, but met empty space. As he turned to look for her, a second explosion blasted the building. "Marissa!" he screamed as he fell to the ground and his world turned completely black.

The dust-filled air was choking him. Brandon tried to move, but his legs were pinned to the floor. "What happened . . . ?" Everything came rushing back and he felt his heart constrict with fear. Marissa! Where was she? Was she hurt? He had to get out of here, he had to find her. Desperation gave him strength and he managed to work his left leg free of the wooden debris he was buried under. He dragged boards and plaster pieces off his body and pushed himself off of the battered floor. The shattered remains around him took his breath away. Only two walls of the hostel still stood. Mounds of rubble filled the lobby as people pried their way free. A small cry caught in his throat when he thought of all the people who had been in the room just minutes before, thought of the one person who meant so much to him. Frantically he started clearing away the spaces where he thought she could be. His fingers were bleeding, cut ragged by plaster and wood, but he kept on. "Marissa," he screamed out. Beads of perspiration slid into his burning eyes and rolled down his neck to soak into his shirt. He felt nothing. "Marissa, where are you?" His heart was throbbing loudly in his ears, drowning out the moans of others.

"Brandon, over here, I'm over here." Her voice was weak as it reached up to him. He saw her waving hand through a small opening within the rubble. She was alive!

Tearing at the boards and debris that held her captive, Brandon pulled her free. He held Marissa tightly, her breath rasping in his ear. "Are you okay?" he whispered, his voice filled with emotion. She laid her head against his chest in answer and he felt his pulse begin to slow.

People moved urgently in the darkness and Brandon could see their silhouettes against the flame-lit night sky. "We need to see if we can help," he said. He led Marissa to the door, afraid to let go of her hand. The street was filled with destruction. Fires burned uncontrolled in building shells and everywhere the sounds of pain reached up through mounds of concrete.

Together, they clawed through the remains to free other trapped victims of the bombing. People joined them and Brandon spotted Dave's tousled head as he bent over to lift a young girl out of the wreckage. His chest was tight as he worked, the sounds of anguish tearing at his mind. As the night grew heavy the rescue workers continued until the last person was freed. Brandon's hands were completely battered, but he never felt more alive in his life. Marissa gazed at him as she tended to an injured woman, her clothes torn and dirt-stained. The smudges of soot on her cheeks and nose only made her more attractive. With a jolt Brandon realized how much she really meant to him. The six years they had been apart had vanished.

"Brandon." Her voice reached out to him, pulling him out of his musing. Whatever else happened, he knew he didn't want to waste one second more of his time with her. Purposefully he strode over to her side and placed an arm protectively over her shoulders. "There's nothing else we can do here," she said softly. "I'd like to try and find some water and wash off this dirt. It should be safe, it looks like the fighting has let up for a while." She looked at him questioningly. "Would you like to come with me?"

Brandon grinned broadly and wiped some dirt off her nose. "Do you think I'm going to let you get away again that easy, lady? No way!" He kissed her warmly. With her arm wrapped around his waist they headed away from the damaged square.

Marissa led the way through the darkened alleys. "Where are you taking me?" Brandon whispered.

"There's a small farm out near the main road. There's a pond there. Hopefully it wasn't touched in this hit and we can wash up there." The smile in her voice warmed Brandon as she took his hand and pulled him with her as she started to run.

The sounds of sporadic gunfire faded as they picked their way through the trees in the darkness. "Are you sure you know where you're going?" Brandon was getting a bit uptight. This was crazy! An owl hooted above him and he jumped nervously in his tracks. Marissa's soft laughter did nothing to ease his tension.

"Come on, it's right down here," she called back to him as she disappeared over the crest of a small hill. Brandon sighed then ran to catch her before he got completely lost.

The sound of water splashing made him turn left at the bottom of the hill. The moon had hidden behind some clouds, so he could barely see his hand in front of his face. "Marissa!" he called out impatiently. Enough of this Boy Scout stuff.

"Oh, God! It's freezing!" she yelled back. She stood knee-deep in the murky water and was brusquely wiping the dirt off her arms and neck.

"Save some for me, will you?" Brandon laughed as he saw her expression. Bravely he took off his shirt and shoes then rolled up his pants. "Here I come!" he shouted as he ran full force into the water, splashing toward her. Marissa screamed and tried to run, but he reached out and grabbed her shirt, pulling her backward into the water. Trickles of water dripped from her glistening hair and streamed down her face. He tilted her head up and kissed her. She rested her forehead against his lips after they parted, then looked up at him, her eyes troubled.

"Marissa, I don't know how to say this. . . ." he began.

"Then don't. Don't say anything, Brandon."

She held her fingers to his lips. He kissed their tips then pulled her into his arms, searching for the words to tell her how he felt. Entwined, they stood silent, lost within their thoughts. The chill of the night air brushed against their wet skin. Marissa huddled closer to him for warmth and slowly he led her out of the still water. He picked up his shirt and handed it to her so she could dry off. She stood looking at the firelit sky, her eyes brimming with tears.

"What's wrong?" Brandon asked, coming up behind her. He wrapped his arms around her and followed her eyes toward the city skyline.

"It's just so crazy. People killing other people over political differences. Sometimes it seems like the entire world has gone crazy." She wiped her eyes and sniffled. "I know it sounds ridiculous for a newsperson to feel this way, but I can't help thinking about all these people, these children without parents, without futures—it kills me!"

"And we're the ones who thrive on the fighting, getting in our latest news flash, waiting for that big break, right?" Brandon turned her toward him and smiled understandingly.

"Exactly. Sometimes I don't know why I do what I do or why it seems so important to me." Marissa frowned. "It's almost as if by being here, covering the fighting, somehow we support it."

"But it's more than that, Marissa. People deserve to hear the truth, see what is really happening. That's what we do. That's what we're here for. And hopefully when the smoke clears, the good guys will have won."

Brandon sat down on the hillside and held his arms open to Marissa. He wasn't sure what the outcome of this conflict would be, but their sources had stated that the government was prepared for a major crackdown. Whatever happened, it wasn't going to be pretty, that he knew.

As Brandon held Marissa close he rested his chin on top of her head, wondering what daybreak would bring. He fought the exhaustion that pulled at him, wanting to savor every minute with her, but as the night crept toward dawn Brandon's eyes grew heavy and Marissa sleepily cuddled against his chest. Her breathing grew steady, lulling Brandon into a light sleep.

It was the silence that awakened him. The first light of morning peeked through the clouds, casting a gloomy gray light over the countryside. He tried to move his arms, but Marissa was lying across him, pinning them to his sides. As he tried to pull free she squirmed restlessly, disturbed by his movements. Brandon smiled. There was something about her that made him feel complete, as though she had become a part of him.

Bending at the waist, he kissed her eyelids. The morning light illuminated her face, making her seem even more beautiful. "Marissa, I don't know where this thing will lead us this time, but I've never felt this way about anyone before. Okay, maybe I felt this way about

my first-grade girlfriend back in Minneapolis,"
Brandon whispered to himself. "What I want to say is, I
mean—well—I love you, Marissa, and I don't want this
to be our only night together." He stared out over the
treetops toward the city, wondering if she felt the
same.

"I love you, too, Superstar." Her voice reached up
to him sleepily. Brandon's skin tingled and his hair
stood on end as he realized she had been awake. He
felt the blood rush to his cheeks and couldn't seem to
find his tongue. She twisted around in his lap and
looked at him, giggling at his obvious discomfort. As
he started to chuckle she reached up and kissed him
lightly. Brandon's heart fluttered. This is it, Walsh,
you've really done it big time, he thought. It didn't matter, though, nothing mattered more than being with
Marissa, right here, right now.

"Something's happened," Brandon said as he
pulled away from her. "There's no gunfire."

Marissa stood up and stretched. She shivered in
the early-morning chill, then gazed out at the horizon.
"I don't see any movement either, it's like everything is
totally still. I think we should go back and check at the
square, see if anyone has any information. Dave's got
to be around somewhere."

Brandon nodded reluctantly, not wanting to leave
the small sanctuary they had found. Marissa started up
the hill toward the woods and stood waiting until he
caught up with her. "Brandon, I just want to say this to
clear the air, okay?" He caught his breath sharply as
she continued. "Whatever happens, happens. I'm
always going to be happy that at least we had last
night." She reached out and caressed his cheek then
turned away, quickly picking up her pace in her eager-
ness to get back. Brandon's chest tightened as he started to jog to catch up with her. Yeah, he had really done
it this time!

■   ■   ■

Brandon found Dave salvaging their gear from the remains of the hostel. He climbed over the mounds of wreckage and helped pull some of the camera bags free. "Anything damaged?" Brandon asked.

"Just a few scrapes and broken lenses, nothing we can't patch up. We moved some of the stuff to a building around the corner last night and got some of the computers working so at least some information could get through. Where have you been all night?" Dave sounded cross, but Brandon noticed the sparkle in his eyes.

"None of your business, Davida!" It slipped out before Brandon realized it and Dave snickered at his blunder.

"Taking Italian lessons, are we?"

Brandon swung at him half-heartedly and missed. "You know, Dave, Marissa and I go back a long way."

"I'm sure you do, Superstar, I'm sure you do!" Dave smirked then reached into a nearby bag and took out a small printout. "You better take a look at this," he said seriously.

"There's been a cease-fire, hasn't there?" He grabbed the paper and read through it quickly.

"Yeah, and it looks like it's going to hold this time. So Cale sent us a message over the wire. Skeeter's gonna be here at high noon to pick us up. We've been reassigned to Beirut. Seems things are getting a bit testy there and the network wants their new superstar to be on the spot. Think you can handle being separated from your Italian tutor?"

Brandon felt the adrenaline rush through his body. "You bet I can," he answered, and slapped Dave's hand in a high five.

"What are you betting on?" Both men turned around as Marissa appeared from behind the remaining battered wall.

"Uh, Brandon, I'll get the gear packed and meet you around the corner," Dave said as he skirted behind her. Brandon shot him a dirty look.

"Well, since there's a cease-fire in effect, Cale decided things are too quiet here so we . . . "

Marissa knew where he was leading. "Got reassigned? Where are you going, Brandon?" Concern was written on her face, but her voice had an edge to it.

"Beirut," he said, confused by her sudden anger. "Skeeter's coming in at noon. What about you? What's up at your end?"

She looked at him squarely and said, "I'm staying here. It seems there's some scheduled talks between the government and the rebel forces. Nothing a superstar like you would want to cover, though."

"You know, Marissa, I don't think you're being fair here." Brandon felt his own anger flaring up. "It's not like I planned this. You know it's not my decision where I go. I would think that you of all people would understand that." His voice was beginning to rise. "And besides, I really don't think this is the time or place to discuss this, do you?" he asked her pointedly. Marissa glanced around at the other people searching through the debris then stared back at him.

"Fine. Where would you like to discuss this, Brandon?" Even though she tried to sound hard, he could sense the tears building. His anger at her reaction faded.

"Why don't you help me get things together here and then we can go out to the field together and wait for Skeeter, okay?"

Her lips trembled, but she managed a twisted smile. "Sure, hotshot, it's your call." As she turned away Brandon finally understood what Dylan had always said about women: the harder you try to make them happy, the more miserable they get.

■ ■ ■

Skeeter landed the prop plane with his usual lack of regard for aviation rules just before noontime. Brandon grinned when he heard the Oklahoman's "yee-haw" as he taxied toward the barn. Marissa stood beside him quietly as they waited for the plane to come to a full stop.

"He's really nuts," Brandon said, half in admiration. The silence between them was driving him crazy, so he found himself rambling. "Dave says there's not a better pilot around, but I really don't think Skeeter's playing with a full deck."

"He's not the only one," Marissa said. She stared off at the countryside.

"Marissa, please don't make this harder than it already is." Brandon reached for her. "I meant what I said last night, you know."

"What?" Marissa's face was blank as she looked up at him earnestly.

"About how much I care for you, and . . . " Brandon seemed to lose his voice.

"And what?" she asked.

He took a deep breath, then proceeded. "And I've never cared about anyone like this before, I swear." He hesitated again. "I do love you, Marissa, remember that. I know it's crazy, but it feels so right this time. No matter what else happens, no one can take away last night. No one." He leaned down and brushed his lips against hers. For just that one minute they were alone, surrounded by emotion.

"Yo, Superstar, you about ready to get this show on the road or what?" Leave it to Skeeter to ruin the moment.

"Be right there, guys," Brandon shouted back. Dave had loaded all the equipment and was already inside the plane. As Brandon turned back to Marissa the propellers began their steady turn, building speed with each revolution. Her eyes swam with tears as

Brandon cradled her face between his hands. "I'll call you at ITN when I get back, I promise, and when I get to Rome, you better be waiting." She kissed him full on the lips, sealing their promise without words.

"Come on, Walsh!" Dave gestured impatiently from the plane.

"I have to go—"

"I know. But please, Brandon, be careful. For me." Marissa held her hands to her chest, a sad smile on her lips.

"Here's looking at you, kid," Brandon saluted her as he bent to pick up his bags. With a broad grin he dashed toward the plane and jumped aboard just as Skeeter started to taxi away. Gathering speed, they quickly lifted off the hardened ground, gaining altitude with each second. Breathless, Brandon sat back in his seat, letting his emotions steady. When Skeeter banked to the southwest, Brandon leaned over and looked intently out the window. There on the ground far below he could see a lone figure standing in the empty field.

"I'll be back, Marissa, I promise," he whispered softly as they flew westward in the bright sunshine.

Brandon was on his feet, Kelly's red baseball cap perched sideways on his head, doing his best Bogart imitation. "I'll be back, Marissa, I promise."

Laughter erupted around him and he twisted his face cavalierly, turning away from the firelight.

"I think the key word here is 'fantasy,' Brandon," Kelly said as she pursed her lips at him mockingly. Brenda cracked up, then turned to her brother as he plopped down on the blanket beside her.

"Does Dylan really say that about women?" she asked pointedly.

A sharp jab in his side warned Brandon not to

answer. He jerked away and said innocently, "Say what?" Dylan looked almost angelic as he stared blankly into the fire.

"What I want to know is if you ever see that hot babe again?" Steve smirked suggestively.

"Steve, you are so shallow! Here Brandon has come up with an unbelievable fantasy and all you can think about is whether he gets the 'hot babe' or not. Unreal!" Kelly shook her head in disgust. Donna nodded in agreement and said, "How deep, Steve."

The banter continued as Andrea sat silently, occasionally throwing popcorn into the flames. No one seemed to notice how quiet she'd been since Brandon had started his fantasy.

"Well, Brenda, ready for the hot seat? It's your turn on the stand," Brandon teased. "Let's see what good old hot wheels has in store for us."

Brenda wasn't bothered by his snide remarks. She knew exactly what her fantasy would be. Steve and David chuckled as she smiled tightly at her twin. "At least my fantasy has a touch of reality to it, Brandon. Yours was more like a hallucination." Donna and Kelly snickered gleefully.

Brandon sputtered in protest but no one bothered to listen. All eyes were on Brenda as she moved away from Dylan and started to speak.

"Well, everyone knows how much I loved acting class this past summer, right . . . ?"

Brenda

BRENDA WALSH TRUDGED WEARILY THROUGH
the pouring rain, dodging the multicolored umbrellas
that seemed to be aimed directly at her tired blue eyes.
Life in the Big Apple was definitely a daily challenge.
As she crossed the street a Yellow Cab zoomed by,
sending a shower of rainwater across her legs. With a
small hop she managed to duck into a small doorway
then pulled a tattered copy of *Backstage* out of her
huge bag.

"Two-twenty-six West Forty-sixth Street," she
mumbled as she looked behind her at the soot-covered
numbers above the door. "Where is this place?"
Exasperated, she shoved the paper back in next to last
week's edition of *Variety* and scooted out into the
downpour.

The Samson Theater was located somewhere

between Seventh and Eighth avenues. The ad had stated that open auditions for *Timeless Moments* started at noon, and Brenda knew if she didn't hurry, she wouldn't be guaranteed a spot. With a heavy sigh she ran splashing through the grayish puddles, intent on getting there as quickly as possible.

Jobs were few and far between for actors and Brenda was near her breaking point. She just had to get this part, it was perfect for her! Sure, it was a small role, but it was the only one that seemed promising right now—the only one that might pay her bills. She scrunched her forehead as she thought of her early days in New York City, when she foolishly believed that everything would come easy. Even though times were rough, she refused to give up and head back to Beverly Hills. She'd rather die than hear her brother say "I told you so." Between Brandon and Dylan, she didn't know which one was worse. At least Dylan didn't really say much about her lack of work. Since this past Christmas, though, Dylan didn't say much at all.

Brenda brushed her long bangs off her forehead and heaved a sigh of relief when she spotted the sign for the theater. This was it. As she walked toward the entrance she wrung the water out of her drenched hair and then combed her fingers through it quickly. Pursing her lips and taking a deep breath, she reached for the door. Here goes, she thought as she entered the darkened theater, one more time.

The applause continued steadily after the curtain closed and Brenda stood hidden in the dark folds of velvet, letting it roll over her. The show was a hit, she could feel it deep inside her. She had watched the performance from the wings and had seen the enthusiasm growing in the audience. She crossed her fingers and silently prayed that the reviews were just as positive.

As people started to mill around backstage she gathered her skirts up and headed for the small dressing room that she shared with two other actors. Carefully she stepped over the lighting cables snaking across the floor.

"Hey, Brenda, there's some guy out front, says he'd like to see you if you've got a few minutes," one of the stagehands called out as she swept past.

"Who is it?" she asked, curious. She hadn't expected any of her friends to come tonight and she definitely hadn't mentioned the opening to her parents; she was too superstitious.

"How should I know? What do I look like, a secretary?" The stagehand sauntered off as Brenda shook her head in frustration. Well, whoever it was would just have to wait until she got changed, she thought as she pushed her way through the crowd of well-wishers.

Discarded costumes were scattered across the tiled dressing-room floor, but Brenda didn't mind. She was relieved that the other girls weren't there chattering about the play. All she wanted was to get out of her costume and into a comfortable pair of jeans. It always amazed her how tired she was after a performance, even if her part was very small. She pulled her pants on then slipped into an old sweatshirt and sat down in front of the arched makeup mirror. The jar of cold cream was almost empty, so she stuck her hand in deep to scoop it out and then slathered the cream over her face, rubbing her cheeks softly. Humming to herself, she went over the entire performance again in her head.

"Excuse me, are you Brenda Walsh?"

Brenda jumped in her chair and turned toward the half-closed door, large gobs of cold cream spattered across her face. "Who are you?" Her heart was racing as she looked at the dark-haired stranger peering in the doorway.

"Terry Simpson. I'm a casting director out in L.A. Do you mind if I come in and talk to you for a few minutes?" He seemed rather harmless in his rumpled tweed suit coat and scuffed cowboy boots.

"Oh, sure, um, I guess so." Brenda scooted out of the chair and opened the door wide. "Brenda Walsh, pleased to meet you." She held out her hand stiffly then quickly pulled it away when she realized it was covered with cold cream. "Sorry . . . I was just taking my makeup off." She shrugged sheepishly and gestured toward her mirror.

"No need to apologize, I'm the one who's intruding. I sent a message back, but I guess you didn't get it?" He looked directly into her eyes as if he was somehow sizing her up.

Her cheeks burned as she looked down at her stockinged feet. "Actually I did, but"—she giggled nervously—"I figured whoever it was could wait." She smiled at Terry, not sure what else to say. He grinned back, then glanced around the cluttered space. "It's not normally this messy in here, but the other girls must have been in a hurry to get out to the party," Brenda explained as she gingerly picked a dress up from one of the chairs. "Have a seat, I just want to take this goop off."

Her mind was racing as she sat down at the dressing table, wondering what this man could possibly want with her. Keep your cool, don't ever let them see you sweat, she thought as she crumpled a used tissue and grabbed another. She leaned forward and scrutinized her visitor through the mirror as he scoped out the dressing room then turned his attention back to her.

"So, how did you like the show?" she asked innocently. The heavy silence was making her more nervous.

"I thought it was good. There were some rough

spots that need to be tightened, but overall, the presentation was quite strong." He seemed to hesitate before he continued. "The reason I wanted to speak with you is that I was very impressed with your interpretation of Elizabeth and I feel you have a strong stage presence."

Brenda smiled at him gratefully through the mirror. "Thank you."

"And I wanted to talk to you about this movie I'm casting for Talon Pictures out in L.A. The female lead is still open and I think you may be just the type of actor we've been searching for." Terry looked at her expectantly.

Brenda swung around on her chair, trying to keep from jumping up in excitement. "Are you talking about the lead in *Too Many Choices?*"

"As a matter of fact, yes. Are you interested in doing a reading for us?" he asked.

"Interested, are you kidding! I would kill for that part!" Brenda shot up out of her seat. "Just tell me when, where, and what; I'll be there."

Terry chuckled at her reaction. "Well, this isn't much notice, but how about tomorrow at noon? I need to grab the four o'clock flight back to the coast, so I'd like to be able to tie up some loose ends beforehand." He reached inside his jacket then handed her a business card. "I'm staying at the Regency. You can stop by on your way home tonight and pick up the script; I'll leave it with the concierge in your name. Then you'll be able to look through the material by tomorrow. We'll just do one scene, so don't worry about learning all the lines. It'll be a loose reading." He clasped his hands firmly as if everything was settled. "Oh, before I forget, the production office is on Broadway above Fiftieth. I'll leave the address for you with the script. Any questions?" He stood up and straightened out his jacket.

"No, I think you've covered it all." Brenda gazed up at him then brushed her hair away from her eyes.

"I'll be there at twelve sharp, ready to go." She followed her guest to the door, clutching his business card in her sweaty hand. "Uh, Mr. Simpson, can I just ask you one question?"

As he opened the door he turned back toward her. "Sure, shoot."

"Why me? I mean, there's plenty of actors out there that would die for this role." Brenda's face was shrouded in doubt as she thought of some of the hottest actors currently working on the screen.

Terry stood silent for a minute. "It's hard to put my finger on it, Brenda, but you have this unusual quality to your work that screamed to me of Cassie." He laughed at her expression of disbelief. "I mean it; I really think you are perfect for the part. So I guess we'll see tomorrow if I'm right, hah?" He held out his hand, and this time they shook warmly.

"Mr. Simpson, I hope that you're right and that tomorrow will be just the beginning. Thanks a lot for hanging around and coming back to see me." She eagerly grabbed the doorknob to keep her legs from collapsing.

"It was a pleasure seeing you perform, Brenda, and you were definitely worth the wait. I'll see you tomorrow." He tipped his hand in a half salute then walked down the darkened hallway. Brenda watched silently as he disappeared into the night then closed the door softly.

"Yes!" she screamed as she did a frantic two-step in the middle of the floor. "I can't believe it! This is too unreal, I can't believe I've actually got an audition for the part of Cassie Ross!" Brenda caught her breath and looked at herself in the full-length mirror across the room. "Looks like this could be your big break, kiddo!" she said to her reflection. As she gazed into the glass anxiety overtook her. "Just don't screw it up," she half whispered. With a skip and a hop she reached down for her bag and started to pack up her costume. She'd have to put in a quick appearance at the opening party, there was no way out of it. But her mind was no longer on the play. Brenda was counting the minutes until she could escape and pick up the script that was waiting for her at the Regency Hotel. With a cursory glance in the mirror she hitched her bag on her shoulder and set off for the street to flag down a taxi.

"Ladies and gentlemen, we should be landing in approximately five minutes. At this time we ask that your seats and tray tables are in their closed, upright positions."

Brenda shut her eyes tight, trying to will away the butterflies eating at her stomach. She wanted to pinch herself to make sure she wasn't dreaming. Last week she had read an article in *Variety* about the casting problems on *Too Many Choices*. Now here she was on her way to Los Angeles after signing on for the female lead. She smiled to herself as she recalled her conversation with her parents the evening after her audition.

"Mom, I got the part."

Brenda's mother had screeched in delight and shouted for her husband. "Jim, Jim, she did it! Brenda got the part!" Brenda giggled excitedly as she heard her father's hoots of encouragement echoing in the background.

"I knew she would. Way to go, Brenda, that's my girl!"

"Honey, did you hear your father?" her mother asked.

"How could I not hear him, I'm sure half the neighborhood did." Brenda smiled warmly into the phone. "So, I'm flying out to Los Angeles on Monday. Production doesn't start for about six weeks, but the production company wants to do a round of press conferences to build up advance PR on the film.

"Brenda, that's wonderful! We are so thrilled for you." Cindy Walsh's voice was muffled as she relayed the information to her husband. "What time does your flight land? Should I meet you at the airport?"

"No, Mom, I think that everything's been taken care of. Once I have some idea of what my itinerary is, I'll call you, okay?" Brenda knew her parents would expect her to stay at home while she was in town, and it was difficult for her to explain that things might be different now that she had this role. Not wanting to get into any confrontations with her parents over it, she quickly shifted gears. "Have you talked to Brandon?" she asked innocently.

"He called last night and we told him how you had gotten an audition. He said to tell you break a leg! He'll be so happy for you." Her mother rambled on about how wonderful it would be to have her in town and Brenda listened silently. Sometimes it was so hard to make her parents see that she wasn't a little girl anymore.

"Mom, listen, I just wanted to let you know how it went, but I have to go down to the theater now to tie up some loose ends. I'll call you as soon as I have a better idea of what's going on, okay?" Brenda didn't wait for a response. "Give Dad my love, and when you talk to Brandon remind him that he owes me dinner, all right? I'll talk to you soon, bye." As she hung up the phone Brenda had shook her head and thought about how some things just never changed.

Now, as she sat waiting for the plane door to open, she realized her entire life was changing by the minute. She glanced at the schedule the publicity rep had sent and saw that she was free until the following day. Apparently someone from Talon would be at the airport to greet her and escort her to her room at the hotel. She wanted nothing more than to soak in a hot bath and spend some time going over her lines. She'd deal with her mother in the morning.

Passengers surged forward as the door opened and Brenda reached up for her nylon carry-on bag. The luxuries of first-class flying were something she could definitely get used to. With a light step she waltzed out the doorway and worked her way up the carpeted corridor to the gate.

"There she is!"

"Brenda, Brenda, over here!"

"So how does it feel to have landed such a plum role?"

The blinding flashes and barrage of questions caught her off guard. She stood blindly in the doorway until she could get her eyes to focus on something other than the red spots dancing in her brain. "What?" she asked, confused.

Suddenly the crowd of reporters parted and a petite, older woman dressed in a crisp black business suit grabbed her arm protectively. "Okay, guys, give me a minute with Brenda and then we'll give you about five minutes of questions and photos. Sound fair?" It wasn't a question and the reporters stood back as the silver-haired woman led Brenda off to a small waiting area.

"Sorry about that, I had to call the office or I would have met you at the entrance to prep you. Sheila Sayers, publicity director for Talon Pictures. I'll be with you for the next three weeks or so, getting you some press opportunities and making sure that things are handled appropriately." Her sharp blue eyes darted through the crowd as she waited for Brenda to comment.

"Sounds good to me," Brenda said pertly. Sheila had the air of a woman who knew the ropes and Brenda was grateful she was there. "What should I say to these people?" she asked.

"Just let them ask their questions, keep it light, don't make any definite comments on the production itself. Smile a lot, and above all—be vague. Everyone loves a little mystery." Sheila ran her manicured fingers through her wavy, silver hair. "You look good," she said, checking Brenda over. "Casually comfortable and confident. This should be a breeze. Ready?"

Brenda straightened her shoulders and held her head high. "As ready as I'll ever be." She licked her full lips once then moved forward as Sheila cleared the way for her into the mob.

"Brenda, so tell us how you feel landing the part of Cassie Ross?"

Brenda smiled broadly and laughed. "Like it's a dream!" She turned to the next question smoothly as some of the reporters joined in her laughter.

"Brenda, is it true that you were only playing a small role in the Broadway production of *Timeless Moments* when you were spotted by the casting director?" The reporter waited with his pen poised for her answer.

"I know it sounds like a cliché, but that's exactly what happened. I even made Terry wait because I had no idea who he was. Of course, after he told me, I almost died!" Brenda's face flushed prettily and flashes exploded around her.

"So Brenda, this is a homecoming for you, isn't it?" The question came from the back of the crowd and she couldn't locate the source.

"I moved to Beverly Hills when I was still in high school. I'm originally from Minnesota, though. But yeah, I guess you could say this is a homecoming. My family still lives here." Sheila caught her eye and nodded, signaling that the five minutes were up.

"Well, I have to head out for the hotel now," Brenda explained to the group. Several of the men moaned in disappointment and she giggled at them. "I'm sure I'll be seeing a lot of you these next few weeks." She wiggled her fingers airily and turned away, taking her bag from Sheila's arm.

"So how'd I do?" she whispered eagerly as she walked down the corridor with the older woman.

"Excellent, a real pro. They loved you." Sheila looked at her appreciatively. "Now I see what Terry was raving about all last week. You're quite a find." She placed her arm around Brenda's waist familiarly and squeezed. "I think that you and I are going to have a very good relationship these next few months."

Brenda grinned at her thankfully as they made their way to the entrance. "Did you have any other luggage?" Sheila asked.

"No, I figured a few outfits for now would be fine, and if I needed something, I could always go shopping. I love to shop in Beverly Hills!" Brenda chuckled as she thought of Kelly and Donna and how they used to spend hours in some of the boutiques on Rodeo Drive. Now she could actually afford to buy something. She knew exactly what her first major purchase would be— a Nicole Miller dress that she had been drooling over at Christmas. She was trying to describe it to Sheila when a figure coming through the automatic doors stopped her short.

"Dylan . . ." she said, stunned.

"Who?" Sheila followed Brenda's eyes and raised her eyebrows. A trench coat was casually draped over what looked like a houndstooth Armani suit that seemed tailored to the young man's body. His light brown hair was swept back, stylishly short but with a bit of attitude mixed in. Sheila couldn't stop from staring at him, his warm brown eyes seemed to lure her in. This was definitely one man who was a rare breed!

Brenda stood still, waiting for Dylan to get closer. He seemed preoccupied, not even looking where he was going. Her heart started to pound as he approached. What if he was with someone? she thought, panicking.

She hadn't spoken to Dylan since she had been home for the holidays and they had decided to see other people because of the distance. Of course, Brenda didn't have time to date in New York—she was always working or going on auditions—but Dylan had plenty of free time. Dylan always had time for the ladies, that was the biggest part of their problem.

"Aren't you going to say something to him? Whoever he is, he's definitely someone I'd want to talk to if I were you." Sheila nudged her softly.

"Yeah, of course." Brenda wished she felt half as confident as she sounded. "Dylan!"

He stopped and turned toward them, his face blank until his eyes found her. "Brenda! I can't believe it!" As she rushed over to him Dylan dropped his briefcase and scooped her into his arms. "Hey, babe, how ya doing?" he murmured as he rubbed his face into her hair, smelling its sweet familiar scent.

"Dylan, I can't believe you're here. Did you know I was flying in today?" She looked up at him eagerly.

"I had no idea, Bren. I was just heading for 'Frisco to see a client." He leaned down and kissed her softly on the lips then held his head against hers. "It is sooo good to see you!"

"I hate to break up such a beautiful thing here, but Brenda, we need to get you to the hotel." Sheila stood at Brenda's side and smiled widely at Dylan.

"Who's this?" he asked.

Brenda pulled away and grabbed Sheila's hand. "This is Sheila Sayers. She's a publicity director with Talon. You know I just signed on to do a movie with them, right?"

Dylan smirked. "Yeah, I think I might have read something about that in the paper, Bren. Maybe, I'm not sure, though." He ducked as she swatted at him. "I'm Dylan McKay, how ya doing?" He towered over Sheila as she quickly shook his hand. "Now, Sheila, I know that you have things that you have to take care of, but see, you have to understand something about me and Brenda, okay?"

Sheila found herself nodding at Dylan, though she sensed he was going to outmaneuver her in some way.

"We have this bond, you see, and whenever we're around each other, we need to spend some Q time alone. Do you know what I mean?" He cocked his head. "So how about you go on to wherever you have to go and I'll be sure to get Brenda settled in. Sound good?" He raised his eyebrow seductively and waited.

"Well, Mr. McKay, you are definitely a smooth operator." Sheila chuckled in admiration. "Brenda, the room is all set for you and we really don't have much to go over tonight. How about we meet for lunch tomorrow at noon?"

"Thank you so much, Sheila, you're a doll!" Brenda shouted gleefully. "I'll see you tomorrow in the hotel lobby then." Impulsively she leaned over and kissed the other woman's cheek. "Thanks for everything . . . this really means a lot to me."

Sheila winked. "It would mean everything to me, too, if I were in your shoes, sweetie." She gestured at Dylan suggestively and Brenda cracked up. "Tomorrow then," Sheila said as scooted off, not looking back.

Brenda grabbed Dylan's arm and gazed up happily at him. "So where to now? I really can't believe that we ran into each other like this . . . it's so unreal!"

Dylan laughed. "Yeah, my client's going to think it's unreal, too, when he gets a message that I'm not coming. Listen, I have to make a few calls before we go anywhere. Some details I've got to take care of. It'll just be a few minutes, okay?"

He kissed Brenda's nose lightly and set off in search of an available phone booth. Brenda sat down on a bench and watched as he spoke animatedly into the phone, writing sporadically in a small notepad he had pulled from his trench coat. She hugged her knees happily as she waited, thrilled at the thought of spending time with Dylan. After a few minutes of conversation he hung up the phone and came over to her, a half grin on his face. A lock of hair had worked its way across his forehead and his eyes had a mischievous look.

"What are you up to?" Brenda asked suspiciously. She always got a little nervous when Dylan had that gleam in his eye.

"Who, me?" he said innocently. "I just had my secretary clear my appointments then tied up a few loose ends." He grabbed her hands and lifted her off the bench. "So where would the lady like to go? Do you want me to take you to the Wilshire or would you prefer to go to the beach with an old friend?" He shoved his hands in his pockets and peered down at her.

"Dylan . . . you know I'd rather go to the beach with you, but what about our last conversation? Um, you know, how you said you felt we should see other people . . ." Brenda wanted to clear the air, but didn't know how to begin.

"Yeah, what about it?" He waited for her to speak.

"Well, are you?"

"Am I what, Bren?" His voice rose in exasperation.

"Are you seeing anyone else?" she said quickly, then closed her eyes.

"Oh, that's it." He chuckled. "Brenda, look at me. No, open your eyes and look at me."

She looked at him squarely, folding her arms across her chest. "All right, I'm looking at you," she said defensively.

"I am not, nor have I been, involved with any other woman since Christmas. Okay?" His voice softened as he spoke then he reached out and pulled her to him. "There's only one person I want to be with and she happens to be in my arms right now." Brenda's lips met his eagerly as she wrapped her arms around his neck. All her doubts slipped away as she ran her fingers through his wavy hair.

"Bren, I think we better get out of here, people are starting to stare," he whispered as he nuzzled her neck. She giggled and glanced around the airport mezzanine.

"Where did you park your car, Dylan?"

"I left it in the garage; I figured it was only a short trip. Must be psychic or something." He snorted. "Come on, let's go." He slid her bag off her shoulder then, holding her hand tightly, led her through the automatic doors out toward the parking garage.

The salty air whipped through her long brown hair as they drove along the Pacific Highway in Dylan's red Mercedes convertible. Brenda held her face up to the fading sunlight, basking in its warmth. The sounds of the La's singing "There She Goes" over the CD player made her think back to when she had first left for New York. Dylan hadn't understood why she needed to try acting, but he didn't hold her back. Over the past ten years they had managed to stay in touch, seeing each other whenever they could, but it wasn't easy. Long-distance relationships were definitely the pits! Brenda frowned when she thought about their confrontation at Christmas again. "So how come you aren't seeing anyone?" she asked abruptly.

Dylan glanced at her, then locked his eyes on the winding road. "I couldn't seem to find anyone that held my interest," he said firmly.

Brenda smiled smugly. Serves him right, she thought.

"What about you? No one waiting back in New York?" he asked.

Her complexion darkened as she racked her brain for a quick retort. "That depends on what you mean by waiting," she stated.

"Come on, Bren. Let's not ruin a perfectly good time with this stuff. Truce, okay?" He rested his hand on her leg as he gazed at her out of the corner of his eye. "Life's too short to waste time, right? Besides, we're here," he said as he swung the wheel easily to the left and turned into a long circular drive.

"The house looks great," Brenda said as she shut the car door. Perched on a bluff overlooking the ocean, it seemed to be dominated by windows. Large spaces of glass filled the walls from roof to foundation with only a few planks of natural wood in between. A large cedar deck surrounded it, dropping off steeply to the manicured grounds.

Dylan held the front door open for her then whistled piercingly. "C'mere boy! Guess who's here?" A black Labrador retriever came bounding down a hallway and jumped on his chest, knocking him to the floor. "Hey, Hemingway, cool it, man." Dylan tried to hold the dog back from slobbering all over his face, but the dog broke though. Brenda snickered as he wiped the saliva off his cheeks.

"Some things never change," she said dryly, walking back toward the deck. "You still haven't told me what you thought of my landing the role for *Too Many Choices*." She kept her back to him as she looked out over the water.

"I think it's the best thing that could have happened to you, almost. And I think it calls for a major celebration, just the two of us." Brenda smirked as she heard the sharp clink of crystal behind her. "Would you care to join me?" Dylan said formally as he waltzed past her out to the deck with his arms full.

"What have you got there?" she asked as she sat on one of the deck chairs.

"Some sparkling cider, cheese, crackers, and fresh

strawberries. Do you approve?" He smiled as he sat next to her, then opened the cider and poured it smoothly into two glasses. He handed her a glass then picked up the other. "A toast. For the woman who deserves it all and who was born to play the role of Cassie Ross." Dylan hesitated as Brenda eyed him. "And for the woman I just can't live without any longer. *Salut!*" They clinked their glasses and sipped silently. Dylan watched as the sun dipped lower on the horizon, then moved close to her. "Bren, there's something I wanted to ask you, um, I don't know what you're going to say, but I want you to be honest with me no matter what, promise?"

Brenda's throat tightened as she set her glass down. Dylan's face was totally serious and she suspected that whatever he had to say wasn't good. She shifted nervously then nodded for him to continue.

"It's been really tough without you and I thought at Christmas the best thing would be for us to just let go and live our own lives. There's no way it could work out with you being in New York and me being out here on the coast. But since then, I got to see what my life would be like without you, Bren, and I didn't like it." Dylan sighed and reached out to touch her cheek. "I need you and I want you, Brenda. I want to wake up with you every morning, and I want to kiss you good night before you close your eyes. Now that you got this break and everything, you wouldn't have to stay in New York anymore . . . you could be here with me." He stared at her anxiously then gulped some cider and slapped his hands against his knees. "Okay, what I'm really trying to say is that I love you and I don't want to lose you . . . ever." He stopped for a second, pursing his lips. "So what do you say, will you marry me?"

Brenda's jaw dropped open when she realized what he was asking. With a loud squeal she jumped into his lap, knocking his cider onto the wood planking below.

"Yes, yes, yes! Of course, I'll marry you!" She kissed him excitedly all over his face then suddenly pulled away. "You really mean it, don't you?" Her eyes peered intensely into his.

"Yeah, I mean it," he said softly, memorizing every detail of her face. "How about we seal this one with a kiss?" His voice was husky. Smoothly he reached up and drew her down on top of him, his lips caressing her then becoming more assertive. As the sun slipped silently into the water Brenda closed her eyes and whispered his name.

"What a romantic you are, Dylan!" Kelly said, then laughed at his annoyed expression as Brandon and Steve made loud smooching noises against the back of their hands.

"That's just about the most beautiful story I've ever heard." Donna sniffled as she wiped at her eyes.

Dylan smirked at his friends as Brenda pecked him on the cheek then nestled comfortably in his lap.

Brandon snorted, then hit Steve in the arm, pointing at his sister's smug smile. "The picture of matrimonial bliss, wouldn't you say, Sandman?"

"Oh, Dylan, oh . . ." Steve said mockingly in a high-pitched voice, then fell at Dylan's feet and rolled over in the sand, looking up so he could see Dylan's reaction.

Brenda quickly leaned over and poured the remains of some ice cubes over his chest as Dylan laughed softly behind her. "I think you better cool down, big guy," she said, giggling.

With a loud yell Steve jumped to his feet, his arms flailing to brush away the coldness. "That was totally uncalled for, Brenda," he said as he eyed her threateningly. He pulled out his T-shirt and shook it loose, letting the cold water slide down his stomach.

"She figured you'd get the message this way,

Steve. You know, chill!" Kelly smiled sweetly at him as he sat down on the blanket.

"Come on, you guys, let's not start arguing!" David grabbed a bag of popcorn and passed it over to Steve. "Here, have some popcorn." A smile tugged at Steve's lips. With a shrug he grabbed the bag and crossed his legs Indian style in front of the fire.

"Okay, Dylan, your turn," Andrea said quietly.

"Hey, how about going the other way, man?" Dylan looked over at Andrea. "That would make it your turn, Andrea. What do you say?" He winked suggestively.

"Come on, Dylan, stop screwing around," David said curtly, surprising himself. Dylan cocked his eyebrows at him.

"What's the matter, Hobson, can't find the words?" Brandon snickered at his friend's uneasiness.

"Yeah, I have the words, Minnesota, I just don't like sharing them with anybody." Dylan didn't like letting people get close to him and this sort of thing made him real uptight. He shook his head slowly then stopped when he felt Brenda's eyes burning into him. "Okay, okay. No problemo; if it's my turn, it's my turn. I can handle it." Gently he lifted Brenda off his lap, ignoring her cries of protest, and then pulled himself closer to the fire. "So, like, I finished school and took off on my bike for a little R and R. Figured I could see a little bit of this U.S. of A."

Donna turned to David and smiled. Who was Dylan kidding? she thought. From the way he was talking he must think about what to do with his life all the time. Kelly was right, it was the quiet ones you had to watch out for . . . or did she say still waters run deep? Oh well, whatever. With a small shrug she leaned forward and took a soda out of the cooler, never taking her eyes off Dylan.

Dylan

THE RINGING OF THE TELEPHONE PULLED
Dylan out of a deep stupor. Bleary-eyed, he reached
toward the nightstand and knocked over the clock
radio, his hand searching desperately for the receiver.
"Yeah?" he croaked, blinking rapidly.

"This is the front desk, Mr. McKay. You had
requested a wake-up call for seven o'clock." The man's
voice was annoyingly chipper and Dylan grimaced.

"Yeah, thanks," he said lifelessly, setting the
receiver down and rolling over once again. Morning
already, he thought wearily. He opened his eyes and
gazed at the cracked paint that spidered across the
ceiling like a road map. What town was this? he wondered, trying to recall where they had finally decided
to pack it in for the night. Somewhere in Tennessee.

Swinging his legs off the bed, he stretched lazily

then dropped down to the threadbare lime-green carpet and started to do sit-ups. Forty-nine, fifty . . . Dylan grunted as he flipped over and dived into a vigorous round of push-ups. When the sweat beaded on his forehead, he stopped and headed into the bathroom. The tub was small and water-stained, lines of mildew surrounding the tile. He wiped the sides down with a wet washcloth then turned on the shower, feeling the water cautiously before he stripped off his shorts and climbed in. The hot water massaged his skin, and he stood motionless, enjoying the respite from his aching muscles.

Life on the road was rough, but Dylan couldn't seem to get it out of his system. For eight years he'd been doing this circuit, traveling with the racers from track to track, performing his stunts wherever he could. Instead of getting tired of it, he seemed to get drawn deeper into the life, something that Brenda couldn't seem to understand. When he had called her about the initial offers from Testron, she had barely spoken to him. With a tormented sigh he rested his head against his forearm on the wet tile and let the water stream down his back. Dylan didn't know what to do to make Brenda happy anymore. He just had to keep on doing the circuit; at this point there was no turning back for him. He had put too much time into building his reputation to just walk away. It was a tough call, but he just couldn't settle down yet.

"Yow!" Dylan yelled as a burst of cold water hit him and he quickly reached down to turn the faucets off. Grabbing a dingy white towel off the rack, he briskly dried himself off, his mind no longer on his love life but focused on the cramped race schedule ahead. They had about another four hours of hard driving before they reached the track in Indiana and he was anxious to get there. He always liked some downtime before a stunt so he could check out the track, get a feel for the arena.

With a quick glance around the motel room Dylan made a last-minute check for belongings, grabbed his gear, then opened the door and stepped out into the glaring morning sunlight. On the road again, he thought ironically to himself as he headed toward the unpretentious roadside diner across the parking lot. As he anticipated the bacon grease and fried potatoes Dylan's stomach growled loudly, reminding him how long it had been since he had eaten. He picked up his pace and sniffed the air, smelling the strong aroma of fresh coffee.

The deafening roar of the cars running the track faded as the pack rounded a far turn. The audience cheered as the leader, in a flashy red-and-white Chevy, pulled out ahead by half a car length. Dust and the smell of motor oil hung heavily in the warm summer-night air, adding to the heady excitement of stock-car racing. As the racers bore down on the finish line people jumped out of their seats, screaming in anticipation. When the checkered flags came down, the race favorite flew past the flagman, leaving the other drivers fighting in the dust to place behind him.

Dylan stood silently in the center pit area, taking in all the action around him. He loved watching the drivers and their crews as they dealt with whatever problems cropped up during a race. Anything from a blowout to a fried gasket, they were ready to tackle it all. He shook his head in admiration as the race winner, Bobby Tomas, jumped out of his car and slapped his crew chief's hand in a high five. Just one wrong move; that was all it took. If Brenda could only see what these guys did for a living . . . He smirked and walked across the greasy pit, heading for the small trailer set up outside the main gate. After the track was cleared of any debris and his crew had set up the old junkers, it was his turn to entertain the audience. He breathed in the pungent smell of gas and felt a jolt of excitement course through his body. Almost show-time.

The trailer was unlocked and Dylan bounded through the doorway. His stunt crew was moving quickly, not wasting any time, so he knew he only had about twenty minutes before he was on. He pulled his shirt off and opened up the small closet where his cos-tume hung, wrapped in cellophane.

"Yo, D.M.!" The door opened as his stunt coordina-tor, Jack Davis, waltzed in. "Track's pretty dry, not too much oil to worry about. I checked with the manage-ment and they got a head count of about eleven thou-sand. Said it's a bit above average, probably because of the promo we did." He grinned sheepishly when Dylan cocked his eyebrows. "You know, the posters on the telephone poles, that kind of thing. It might not be the big time, McKay, but it works real good in the heart-land!"

Dylan nodded and pulled on his tight black pants then bent down in the closet and searched for his matching boots. "Does the crew know I'm going for twenty tonight?" he said as he threaded his straps through the shining silver buckles.

"Now, Dylan, I don't know if that's the smartest thing to do, man." Jack held his hand up as Dylan start-ed to interrupt. "Just listen to me for a second, will you? I know what you're trying to do and I can under-stand it. But I don't think it's worth risking another injury to prove yourself to a bunch of snob-nosed busi-ness suits. It's not going to help if you're laid up with a few broken bones for the rest of the season, do you follow me?"

"Jack, I know what I'm doing. I know I can top twenty cars in a jump with my eyes closed. Stop being such a girl, will you?" Dylan stood up and looked into the small mirror mounted on the wall. "I haven't missed a stunt in over a year. I think it's time I get a little aggressive." He turned and placed a hand on Jack's shoulder. "And besides, I have the best crew on the circuit to make sure that nothing goes wrong."

Jack snickered and peered at Dylan. "Okay, I won't argue about it anymore, but if you get hurt, don't come crying to me. I think you're asking for trouble here." He shrugged off Dylan's hand and headed toward the door. "I better get out there and tell the crew to round up a few more junkers. I'll check back with you in a little bit." He closed the door firmly behind him as Dylan smiled at his friend's uncalled-for concern. It was going to be a piece of cake; he just knew it.

Dylan ran a comb through his hair quickly then glanced out the window at the racing fans wandering around the concession stands. He was determined to give them something to remember him by tonight. He breathed in deeply and picked up the telephone, dialing Brenda's number by memory. Words of encouragement were what he needed right now. He tapped his fingers on the countertop nervously as he listened to the phone ringing insistently in Beverly Hills.

"Ladies and gentlemen, the world's greatest motorcycle daredevil, Dylan McKay!" The announcer's voice reverberated through the noisy cheers of the crowd as Dylan slipped on his black helmet and waved enthusiastically to the audience. Young girls screamed his name shrilly from the bleachers. With a huge kick, he started the bike and revved the engine, grinning widely behind the helmet lip.

"He will attempt to jump twenty, count them, *twenty* cars with only seventy-five feet of acceleration space, ladies and gentlemen. An amazing feat and one that very few daredevils manage to complete successfully."

The loudspeakers crackled as the prestunt buildup continued.

Dylan gunned the motorcycle for emphasis then took off, circling the track several times. Each time around, he kept his eyes glued to the landing ramp on the opposite side. With a sudden burst of speed he was airborne, flying over the line of cars with the boisterous shouts of the audience ringing in his ears.

"There he goes, he's got incredible height—see how easily he's maintaining his speed. This is unbelievable!" The excitement in the announcer's voice grew. People jumped from their chairs as Dylan reared the front of the motorcycle higher, as if he were riding a bucking stallion. With complete control and amazing gracefulness, he landed on the ramp on his back tire then set the front one down smoothly. He had done it perfectly, he knew by the look on Jack's face as he stood motionless, waiting at the end of the ramp.

Dylan spun the bike around and pulled to a stop at Jack's feet, slipping his helmet off quickly. "So what did you think, big guy?" he asked softly.

Jack laughed out loud and grabbed him around the neck in a bear hug, taking the helmet from his hands. "It was beautiful, absolutely bee-u-tee-ful! You were right," he yelled.

Dylan raised his arms triumphantly and twisted around on his seat, letting the audience cheers surround him. As two crewmen came up on his sides he slid off the bike easily and strolled toward the announcer's stand.

"What a show, ladies and gentlemen." The emcee stood only to Dylan's chin, his white hair sprouting in tufts around his ears. His skin was naturally ruddy and the exertion of announcing made the blood rush to his face, making him look even redder. "Dylan McKay, one of the best daredevils on the circuit today. What went through your head as you pulled off that ramp?"

Dylan hesitated and cleared his throat. "I really don't think too much when I'm jumping. I just listen to the cheers of the crowd, get myself pumped up a little, then give it my best shot." His voice was gravelly, its tone magnified by the PA. Squeals of delight reached up to him from the stands and he grinned widely.

"Well, young man, if that's all it takes, then you are definitely going to have an interesting career in motorcycle stunt jumping. So let's give the man a hand, Dylan McKay, who successfully jumped twenty cars lined up front to rear without breaking a sweat. Amazing!" The older man guided Dylan off the stand easily as the crowd roared. As Dylan reached the bottom stair the announcer switched gears expertly and started to prep for the next race. "Now, ladies and gentlemen . . ."

Still smiling, Dylan strode through the crowd and made his way to the trailer. His progress was interrupted several times by fans asking for his autograph. He quickly wrote his name on the napkins and race programs placed in front of him, making idle conversation with the young girls who stood giggling around him. "How do you spell that?" he asked an attractive blond girl dressed in tight jeans and a faded T-shirt.

"N-A-N-C-Y," she answered breathlessly, swaying in place.

Dylan nodded as he wrote, a smile playing on his lips.

By the time he finished, the sweat had dried on his back and the race had begun, leaving only a few starry-eyed females watching him from a distance. He waved at them, causing an eruption of nervous laughter, then jogged the remaining distance to the quiet solitude of his trailer.

"Hey, Dylan." A man's voice from the doorway caught him off guard as Dylan stood guzzling a bottle of water from the trailer's refrigerator.

"Mr. Grayson, how are you?" Dylan hid his surprise behind a broad smile. "So what brings you to this part of the country?" He gestured for the older man to come in and close the door.

Sam Grayson was an old stock-car racer who had managed to work his way up the ranks of one the largest motor-oil companies in the world. He had the powerful build of a longtime racer, his frame still muscular. He looked younger then his fifty years, clad in faded blue jeans and a bright red sweater, his feet squeezed into a pair of snakeskin boots. "I thought I would do a little market research, see how the audiences relate to your shows, name recognition—you know, that kind of thing. I wanted to tell you how impressed I was out there. You did a terrific job with the jump, worked the crowd just right, and got the ladies screaming." He looked at the window for a second. "I've got a proposition for you, and I think that if we can come to terms on this, it would be beneficial for everyone involved," he said firmly, staring at a photo of Dylan on his motorcycle that hung from the wall. "How would you like to do the Snake River jump?"

"What terms did you have in mind?" Dylan kept his voice even.

"We'll cover all the permits, the setup fees, the cost of modification, and of course, we'll provide the motorcycle. We'll spend over one and a half million on promotion for the stunt, which will help us get network coverage." He pursed his lips, studied Dylan's face, then continued. "And if you complete the jump successfully, we'll give you two million cash. If you don't, one million." He stood still and waited.

"If I don't, I might not be around to collect that one million," Dylan said, with a knowing look. "What about after the stunt? What is Testron prepared to guarantee then?" He sat down in an armchair and put his feet up on the coffee table. He was in control here and he knew it.

"We are prepared to sign you to a spokesperson

contract for twelve months after the successful comple-
tion of the stunt. I don't have figures here with me, but
our spokespeople normally make in the high six figures. Interested?"

"I might be," Dylan answered coolly. "Do you really
think that people remember Knievel's jump over the
Snake River? It's been over twenty years since he tried."

"It was such a media event that even if people have
forgotten, the old footage will surely be aired, and that
alone will pique the public's interest," Grayson said
firmly.

"How wide is it?" Dylan was mapping out the possibilities in his head.

"Just shy of a quarter mile."

Dylan nodded and leaned forward. "So Testron will
buy the bike? I like that. Listen, Mr. Grayson—"

"Call me Sam." He smiled thinly.

"Okay, Sam, you've got me curious. Why don't you
draw up a draft of the agreement, including the
spokesperson stuff, and send it over to my man, Jack
Davis? Give us a week or so to go through it and we'll
get back to you." Dylan set his feet on the floor and
stood up. Pointedly he walked to the door and opened it.

Grayson's face hardened when he realized he was
being dismissed. But he needed to play McKay's
game, whatever it was, if they were going to get this
stunt put together. Casually he shook Dylan's hand
then stopped on the stairway. "Don't take too long now
thinking it over, Dylan, there's always another guy out
there waiting for a break like this," he said with a small
smile as he walked toward his limousine.

Dylan ignored the parting jab and scanned the
racetrack for Jack. When he spotted his coordinator's
black jumpsuit near the grandstand, he cupped his
hands and called out, waving for Jack to come over.
As Jack scooted up the stairs to the trailer Dylan
looked down at him with a gleam in his eyes. "You

are never going to believe who was just here," he said mysteriously. "Jack, this is it, we are talking the ultimate challenge. Numero uno, top of the line! I can't believe they're willing to put up serious buckeroos!"

Completely baffled, Jack allowed Dylan to pull him into the trailer and firmly close the doors against inquisitive ears.

"Yes!"

The motorcycle flew smoothly through the air, allowing Dylan the opportunity to gaze down at the cracked dirt surface of the training center. He closed his eyes and imagined looking down at the meandering path of the Snake River almost eight thousand feet beneath him. With a quiver of anticipation he opened his eyes and landed the bike effortlessly. Another perfect test jump, this one just over seven hundred feet. He raised his fist at the crew members watching from the pit then turned the motorcycle around.

"Piece of cake," he said as Jack ran over. "You know I really think that with the turbo engine, this baby should have no problems making it over. She's so smooth, she purrs." He patted the glistening black gas tank then swung his leg over and jumped off.

"Looks like you had some room to spare there, Dylan. How'd it feel?" Jack scurried along to keep up with him.

"I probably could have gone another seventy-five feet easy." He laughed. "I hope Testron knows what they've gotten into."

"Sam Grayson does. He called about five times this morning, wanting to know the latest test-jump length." Jack shook his head in amazement. "Looks like this is turning out to be a major sports event. Grayson says that 'Wide World of Sports' is going against CBS for broadcast rights. So I wouldn't worry about Testron losing out on this deal, Dylan. If things go the way we planned, they're going to be laughing all the way to the bank."

Dylan stopped. "Yeah, but what if things don't go the way we planned? Then what, Jack?" He knew it was just jitters, but he couldn't help voicing his doubts. Things could go wrong, he had been through it before. Fourteen broken bones and over seven hundred stitches later, he knew that the worst could happen. Each time he jumped, he faced that possibility.

Dylan frowned, then swung his upper body from side to side, stretching his tense back muscles. No need to dwell on the past, McKay, he thought as he listened to Jack go over the remaining test jumps and their setups. He glanced at his watch and saw that it was almost time to call Brenda, and for a brief second he wished that she was there with him. His brow creased as he pictured her wandering aimlessly around the test sight, looking for something to do to fill the dull hours each day while he prepped for the stunt. No, it was best that she stayed in California with her friends, he thought as he headed for his motorcycle to drive into town and call her.

"Hey, Bren, it's me." Dylan shoved his hands into his pockets, feeling the loneliness creep up on him like it did every time he heard her voice.

"Dylan, why didn't you call me last night? I've been so worried about you. Can't you give me a number or something where I can reach you?"

He grimaced at her tone, then tried to avoid another argument. "Hon, I would if I could, but I don't know what the number will be at the trailer once everything gets set up. Testron is taking care of it, so once it's ready, I'll call you, okay?"

Brenda sighed. "I'm sorry, Dylan, I don't mean to

get all over you. I just hate it when I can't talk to you. How are the test jumps going?"

"Pretty good. I landed at over seven hundred today and we haven't modified the bike yet. Looks like everything is on target. How's your family?" Dylan missed Brandon and thought of how cool it would be to have Minnesota here with him. He could use a little of that unending optimism right about now.

"Everyone's fine. Mom and Dad went to Cabo San Lucas with the company, so they won't be back until next week. I haven't talked to Brandon in a while. I'm sure he'll stop by on Saturday." She hesitated. "Dylan, do you want me to fly out there for the jump?"

"No, Bren, it's better for me if I don't have any distractions . . . and with you around, I'm sure I wouldn't get enough rest, you know?" They both laughed knowingly.

"Well, if you change your mind, just call, okay? Listen, Kelly's outside beeping, we're going to this hot new sushi bar out on Sunset. Call me tomorrow, okay? And Dylan, I love you, remember that."

"I love you, too, Brenda. Have a great time and tell Kelly I said hi." He stood there looking at the receiver as the dial tone clicked in then slowly hung up the phone. Not wanting to go back to the emptiness of his small motel room, Dylan hopped onto his bike and headed out to the jump site to watch the sun set over Hell's Canyon.

The jump ramp was silhouetted against the burnt-orange sky, reaching up toward the high clouds. Dylan sat quietly looking out over the horizon, trying to envision how different it would be in one week's time. The only sound filling the silence was the slow gurgle of the river far below. The far side of the canyon was hidden in the evening shadows. Well, there were no two ways about it, he thought. Either he made it or he didn't. Cautiously he peered over the edge and tossed a rock into the darkness. He waited, but heard nothing.

■ ■ ■

The grinding gears whined as the satellite flatbed tried to make its way up the small incline. Jack Davis, dressed in his official uniform, fluttered around the rig, flagging the driver forward. The heat of the midday sun bore down on him as he pulled a faded red bandanna from his back pocket and wiped the sweat off his forehead. He squinted up at the sky, looking for some sign of a break in the unrelenting heat. With a curse he headed toward the white double-wide trailer Testron had provided for their use.

"Ah, Mr. Davis. How's everything going?" Sam Grayson stuck his head out of the rear window in the air-conditioned limousine.

"Fine. Everything is fine," Jack sputtered, and continued on his way. Grayson seemed intent on making his life miserable until this stunt was over. Jack had a feeling that it was more than monetary concern that made Grayson so overbearing. Something about Dylan appeared to bring out the worst in the old coot. Serves him right, coming here and throwing his weight around. With a shrug he opened up the trailer door, sighing as the cool air embraced him.

"What's up, Jack?" Dylan asked. He was sprawled out on one of the tweed couches, reading a motorcycle magazine.

"Grayson is here already, prowling around. What did you ever do to get his nose out of joint?" Jack grabbed a glass from the counter and poured himself some iced tea.

Dylan chuckled. "I think I treated him a bit too offhandedly and he hasn't forgot about it yet. No big deal, he'll get over it eventually." He closed the magazine and tossed it on the coffee table. "So how are things going with the setup?" If he was nervous, Dylan hid it well.

Jack stared at him. "Are you okay? You've been pretty low-key about this all week."

"I'm cool, Jack, believe me. I really think that this stunt is going to be pure and simple." He smirked. "See, I have something that Evel didn't have."

"What's that?"

"You." Dylan pointed at the older man.

Jack swung at his finger, then sat down heavily in a recliner. "One thing for sure, it's a scorcher out there. Ninety-nine in the shade at least. There's a couple thousand spectators lining up on both sides already and luckily some concessionaires had the foresight to get work permits for the event. Otherwise the audience would be dropping into the canyon, not you." He took a large gulp then set his glass down on an end table. "The network has everything almost ready to go. I helped get the satellite truck in place. Guy doesn't even know how to drive a flatbed, grinding his gears like crazy, thought he was going to drop the trannie right there."

Dylan snorted then asked, "What time do I have to be out there by?"

"You've got about forty-five minutes. They want to do a prestunt interview and then I think they're going to run the old tape on Knievel. By that time you'll be ready to go. Sound good?" Jack leaned toward Dylan.

"Yeah, sounds great. I was just thinking about how Knievel must have felt, knowing all those people were watching. Man, talk about the ultimate letdown!" His brown eyes took on a glazed look. "If for some reason I don't make it, Jack, I want you to be sure to take care of everything like I told you."

"Come on, D.M., is that any kind of talk? You've managed to breeze through all the test jumps. This will be the easiest stunt you've done!" Jack slapped Dylan's arm enthusiastically. "Why don't you take a long, hot shower or something and relax a bit, huh? I'm going to do a final check over on the bike and the ramp spacing

then I'll come back and get you for the prejump interview." He stood up, pulling down the legs of his jumpsuit. "Putting on a few pounds in my old age," he said
lightly, then opened the door and set out in the stifling
heat.

Dylan didn't move from the couch. He stared at
the melting ice cubes in Jack's glass and went over the
routine one more time in his head. Four full revolu-
tions for speed around the acceleration track then one
hundred and fifty feet of ramp space, punch in the tur-
bos, and fly. The height and speed of the jump should
give him about seven feet to spare on landing, he figured. Then, with a bit of luck, he'd be on his way back
to Beverly Hills within hours. No problemo!

As his pulse started to race Dylan got up from the
couch and pulled off his T-shirt distractedly, slipping
into a faded black one that matched his weathered
leather jacket. His jeans were charcoal-colored, completing the hard-as-nails look he had become known
for. Dipping his hands under the faucet, Dylan ruffled
the top of his hair, creating fresh spikes, then
smoothed down his sideburns. One more thing, then
he was ready.

He grabbed the phone off the counter and
punched in a string of numbers. As the line connected,
his mind wandered back to the layout of the jump.

"Hello, Walsh residence." Brenda sounded tense.

"Hey, Bren, it's me." Dylan cradled the phone
between his shoulder and chin as he lifted himself up
onto the countertop. "I just wanted to give you a call
before everything got too crazy. How're ya doing?"

"Dylan, I'm so glad you called! I'm a nervous
wreck! I've been watching the previews all afternoon
with Kelly and Donna. How are *you* holding up?" she
asked in a concerned tone.

"I'm okay. I just kind of hung out all morning. I've
been trying to keep my mind occupied so I don't stress

out completely, y'know? Jack said everything is on target, though he's freaking about the heat. Did you see, it's over a hundred degrees here?" He chuckled then peered out the window from his perch and noticed the crowd had multiplied. "No wonder they call it Hell's Canyon."

"Dylan, are you sure you want to do this? You don't have to go through with it if you don't want to." He could hear the tears behind her wavering voice. "What if something goes wrong, what if you don't make it?"

"What if, what if, Bren. Come on, where's your faith? This is Dylan we're talking about here. You know I can pull this off easily. Then I'll have the contract with Testron and maybe I won't have to go back on the stock circuit anymore." He knew that the only way to convince her this risk was worthwhile was to throw in the possibility of a commitment down the line. "You said you didn't know how much longer you could put up with my being on the road anyway. Well, this is my opportunity to get out of it once and for all. I've got to give it a shot."

"Oh, please! I know you, Dylan, and I know that the only reason you want to do this so bad is because you want to succeed where someone else failed—it has nothing to do with financial security!" Her tone grew edgy. "In some ways you are exactly like your father."

Dylan flinched then gritted his teeth. "Just what is that supposed to mean?"

"Face it! You're both risk takers, always trying to come out on top, no matter what the risk or who gets hurt along the way. Look where it got him, Dylan." She started to cry openly.

Jack McKay was still on probation after doing time for fraud and insider trading, and Dylan's relationship with his father remained cool and distant at best.

"My father has nothing to do with this, Brenda.

This is for me, this is something I need to do. I'm sorry that you can't see that." The sound of her sniffling tore at him and he felt his anger slipping away. "Don't cry, Bren. I just called to tell you how much I miss you and that I love you."

"I love you, too, Dylan, but I get so scared, thinking about what could happen to you. Promise me you'll be careful?"

He closed his eyes and nervously ran his fingers through his hair, wishing he could ease the pressure building up in his head. "I promise."

"When will you be home?" she asked.

"It'll be late. I'll stop by on my way from the airport, all right?"

"I'll wait up," Brenda whispered.

"Make sure you watch on TV," he said huskily. "I'll see you soon." As he hung up the phone Dylan caught his breath at the sharp pang of loneliness that spread across his chest.

The motorcycle was shrouded by a large gray tarpaulin and stood off to the side of the jump ramp. Swinging his helmet carelessly by the strap, Dylan wandered across the grounds through the work area, pausing periodically to shake hands with several crew members who stopped to wish him luck. The sun was sloping to the west, the arid air cooling quickly. A temporary wooden picket fence had been placed along the edge of the canyon, keeping the thousands of spectators away from the dangerous drop.

"Slow down, McKay!" Jack's voice reached up over the noise of the crowd. Dylan turned and waited for him, then continued walking as Jack gave him the final rundown.

"The engines were greased, fueled, and tested; no

problems there. Both ramps are in place and the sun shouldn't be a problem glare-wise. Do you have your goggles?" Jack looked suspiciously at Dylan's leather jacket.

"I've got my shades in here," Dylan answered as he patted his coat pocket.

"Dylan, how many times do I got to tell you! You know you should be wearing safety goggles on a jump like this!" Jack admonished.

"Don't worry, man, nothing's going to go wrong, I promise." Dylan grinned at him assuredly as they approached the covered motorcycle. With a self-confident pull he tugged the covering off and whistled in admiration. "Looking good, looking good," he said as he circled the modified bike. With twin turbo engines and miles of chrome, it looked like something straight out of a science-fiction flick. "You did a great job, Jack, thanks." Dylan turned to his stunt coordinator and smiled.

"Heck, it was nothing. With all the money that Testron was willing to throw our way, we could have built you a goddarn plane!" He shrugged off Dylan's compliment uncomfortably. "Let's just see if it gets you to the other side," he added quietly. Jack squinted as he looked out at the far wall of the canyon, where blurry dark figures lined the edges of the fence.

Dylan threw his arm around the other man's shoulder and squeezed him tight. "It will, man, trust me. How about you meet me at the other side, hah? We can celebrate our new and everlasting relationship with Grayson and the boys." Dylan chuckled at Jack's expression.

"Do we have to deal with that pain in the—"

"Uh, uh, uh. Don't say it. He can be a real charmer when he lets go of himself." Dylan laughed heartily. "Well, I guess it's showtime, wish me luck." He pulled out his black sunglasses and put them on. Jack watched silently as Dylan slipped on his helmet and climbed on the bike.

"Knock 'em dead, kid," Jack said, his eyes tearing as he leaned over and punched Dylan in the arm lightly. He stared at Dylan for a minute than walked toward his spotting position at the top of the jump ramp.

The motor started instantly and the crowd grew silent at the sound of the huge engine revving, echoing against the canyon walls. Dylan looked around at the expectant faces and smiled to himself. No turning back now, McKay, he thought as he pulled away from the work pad. Adrenaline shot through his body as he completed the fourth revolution on the acceleration track. The high-pitched shrieks of female fans rang through his helmet. Picking up speed, he drove effortlessly through the far turn, the expectant faces of the crowd becoming a color-drenched blur as he flew past. As he rounded the final curve Dylan looked up toward the top of the ramp, held his breath, and pressed forward. With a burst of power the turbo engines came alive just as he left the top of the jump ramp and became airborne. Completely motionless, he kept his eyes level as the opposite side of the canyon loomed ominously in the evening shadows. The wind whipped past his face, but Dylan didn't notice. The sound of blood coursing through his body roared in his ears, the only indication of how scared he was. Just one small move could break the momentum he needed. His eyes began to burn as sweat streamed off his forehead. Just a little further, that's all he needed and then he'd be home free. Just a little more . . .

The motorcycle suddenly started to drop from its arch about three quarters of the way across the canyon. Gunning the engine desperately, Dylan realized that it was going to be more than a close call this time. The audience cheers grew in volume as he drew closer to the landing ramp, fighting hard for each additional foot.

Dylan panicked. He quickly turned to see where he was and found himself looking straight down into the riverbed, eight thousand feet below. His scalp tingled as his hair stood on end. With a desperate jerk he gave the throttle one last blast and pushed with all his might. The nervous shouts of the spectators gave him strength. The motorcycle reared up wildly, shooting past the tip of the ramp, landing several feet down the runway. The roar of the crowd grew thunderous as Dylan breezed down to the pit area where his crew stood waiting with the people from Testron.

Admiration and relief were written all over their faces when Dylan shut off the motorcycle and slipped off his helmet. With a sheepish grin Dylan looked back at the ramp then turned toward where a somber-faced Sam Grayson stood waiting.

"Like I said, no problemo," Dylan said dryly. "So when do I start work?" He smirked at Grayson openly, enjoying the other man's expression of disbelief. Yeah, this was how it felt to be a winner, he thought to himself as he chuckled loudly. Then he turned back to the crowd, waving as the television cameras caught his broad dimpled smile, the dark sunglasses masking his eyes and giving him an air of mystery. He swung around as the cheers swelled to a fever pitch. Yep, this is it, this is where I want to be. Right at the top.

Dylan licked his lips eagerly as he finished, as if he could actually taste the sweetness of his success.

"Cool tale, bro! I can see you doing something like that." Steve reached across the circle and slapped Dylan's hand enthusiastically in a high five as Brandon and David joined in.

"Dylan, I can't believe that you wouldn't want me

there with you!" Brenda's face was stiff with disbelief as she stared at him. "What is the big deal about life on the road anyway? You act like there's some great big mystery to it or something." She shook her head.

"How would you know what it's like, Bren? The longest you've ever been in a car was to go to summer camp and that was only six hours." Brandon snorted, sharing a knowing look with Dylan. "You wouldn't want to be around grease monkeys all the time anyway."

"Brandon, please, I really don't need your advice on this." She turned around and pointed her finger at Dylan. "Don't ignore me."

"I'm not ignoring you," he said, raising his hands defensively.

"My point is this. Wouldn't you get lonely living on the road? Wouldn't it be better if I was with you? Or did you have someone else in mind?"

Dylan was incredulous at how quickly Brenda had forgotten this was only a game. If he didn't do something quick, this was sure to erupt into a major blowout. "Well, you know Bren, it really is a tough lifestyle and I figured you would want to stay home with kids and all." He grinned at her innocently, knowing this would definitely infuriate her.

"Dylan McKay, if you think for one minute that I am going to stay home in an apron and raise the kids, I hate to burst your bubble." She gathered up speed as Kelly and Donna nodded approvingly at her. "These are the nineties, buddy, and a woman doesn't have to give up her own aspirations to be a wife and a mother anymore. Not only do I plan to have both a career and a family, I plan to share my parenting duties with my husband! After all, it's only fair that everything in the relationship is fifty-fifty." Brenda folded her arms and waited for his response.

Dylan stared back at her calmly, furrowing his

brow as if he were considering what she said. "Well, I guess we have a slight problemo then," he said after a moment. Brenda didn't notice what a difficult time he was having keeping a straight face.

"I can't believe you, Dylan," she cried out, exasperated. Grabbing a bag of potato chips, she tapped him over the head several times. "You belong back in the Dark Ages!"

"Hey, hey! Knock it off! I was only kidding," he protested feebly, covering his head with his arms as he tried to ward off her harmless blows.

Everyone laughed loudly as Brenda sat back and watched Dylan peek out cautiously from under his arms. As she turned toward Kelly and Donna she said, "That was so unbelievably funny, Dylan—not!" all three girls yelled in unison then laughed gleefully.

"Hey, it's only make-believe, remember?" Dylan chided as Brenda tried to push him over into the sand.

"Don't you think Dylan's fantasy was really cool?" Brandon said quietly to Andrea as David passed out fresh sodas to everyone. "It was so like him. Can't you just see him, dressed in black leather, riding a big old bike?"

She looked at him blankly and shrugged.

"Hey, what's the matter with you all of a sudden—"

"Come on, Brandon, button your lip, will you?" Donna slapped at his arm impatiently. "It's Kelly's turn."

Brandon eyed Andrea warily as she rested her chin in her palm, her eyes focused on Kelly's wild gestures in the air. What'd I do now? he wondered. With a half shrug he reached for some popcorn and leaned back on his elbows to listen.

Kelly

"THE HEMLINE DEFINITELY NEEDS TO BE AN inch shorter," Kelly Taylor said firmly as she walked a full circle around the base of the model's pedestal. "Bring in the back of the jacket tighter, too, so it's more formfitting. It looks too suburban like this, Nancy." She bunched up some of the material in the back of the magenta blazer then looked into the trio of mirrors. "See what I mean—it's got to be darted."

"Piece of cake. Any other alterations?" Nancy Anderson was Kelly's top tailor. She knew how to follow her boss's often scattered directions and had learned quickly that Kelly seemed to have an inborn sense of what would be tomorrow's hottest look.

"No, I think keeping the line straight and crisp is enough with this number. The color is the major selling point here." Kelly nodded abruptly at the tall, willowy model who climbed down and walked briskly into the curtained dressing area.

"What do we have next?" Nancy grabbed her clipboard and ran her finger down the list of the fall window displays. With only three days left before the changeover, she wanted everything covered.

"The ivory chemise, the yellow trapeze, and that's it," Kelly said as she checked over her master diagram of the display windows. "Did the flower boxes arrive yet?" She had ordered over a hundred wooden boxes fulled with vibrant chrysanthemums to be placed on the floor of the display windows. The plain-faced mannequins would appear to be growing in the midst of a luscious fall garden. Kelly smiled to herself as she pictured the finished displays and knew they would definitely catch a potential shopper's attention.

"André said it would be sometime this afternoon."

"Well, then I'm going to head up to my office and try to catch up on some paperwork. Call me if you have any problems with the trapeze. It should be hemmed to about a quarter inch above the knee, okay?" Kelly gathered up her papers and shoved them into her black quilted briefcase then brushed some stray hairs away from her eyes. "I'll be back down in a bit. Thanks for taking care of everything, Nance."

With a quick wave to the other seamstresses Kelly headed out of the alterations area across the plushly padded mauve carpeting of the central sales floor. She glanced around and noted that each of her sales assistants was occupied with clients. Several other customers wandered leisurely through the various designer-boutique alcoves, where small slate-gray cushioned chairs and antique cherrywood side tables offered casual comfort while viewing the high-cost merchandise. Times were tough everywhere these days, but you wouldn't know it by watching the marble counter of a Taylor-Made store. Kelly smiled approvingly then climbed the spiral staircase to the executive offices, her high heels clicking on the creamy ivory stone.

"Good morning, Ms. Taylor," the receptionist said crisply as she watched Kelly approach. Her rich mahogany desk added a necessary touch of warmth to the austere gray waiting area. A large crystal vase filled with tiger lilies sat on a low cocktail table, perfuming the air with their soft heady scent.

"Good morning, Marie," Kelly answered as she strode down the carpeted hallway toward her office. Distant phones rang behind several closed doors and low voices alerted Kelly that it was business as usual up here in the corporate office. She swiftly opened the door to her office suite, eager to get started on the day's work.

"Hey, Barb, how's it going?" She smiled warmly at her fashionably dressed executive assistant. Barbara Stevens had worked with Kelly for almost eight years now, acting as a salesclerk, packer, alterations person, and secretary—often at the same time. When things were real tight at the beginning, she had even gone into competitors' stores and persuaded shoppers to stop in at Taylor-Made. Life without Barb would have been a living nightmare, Kelly knew.

"Kelly, you would not believe the morning we've had up here. Let me tell you, if something doesn't give soon, I'll have to find me a place for a permanent vacation. Someplace warm, without any telephones and plenty of young, muscular, and totally available men." Barbara guffawed and handed over a wad of pink phone-message slips. "That's just the past half hour, boss lady, the others are in on your desk. I'll give you a few seconds before I come in." She swiveled around in her chair and started tapping away on the computer keyboard, her scarlet-colored nails shining in the harsh overhead light.

Kelly watched for a minute then walked into her office and closed the door softly. Papers covered the huge oak desk that was surrounded by two walls of windows. Hurriedly Kelly sifted through the piles, pulling out several reports. She collapsed into her deep rose-colored leather chair then read through the phone messages, separating them into two small piles.

"Call, have Barb handle, call, have Barb handle, call—" Kelly stopped and read the message she held in her hand again. "Kyle Lenay. Well, wouldn't you know it? I wonder what's so important that he could actually break down and call me?" Six months had passed since Kelly had walked out on him. She no longer felt the burning pain when she thought of him, but she knew it wouldn't be the smartest move on her part to call him back. Still, she was curious. Kyle could still get under her skin. Nervously she picked up the receiver and dialed his number from memory.

"Lenay Designs, good morning."

"Mr. Lenay, please," Kelly said in a businesslike tone.

"One moment." The line was filled with the sounds of classical music for a split second.

"Mr. Lenay's office."

"Samantha, how are you? It's Kelly Taylor," she said cheerfully. She had always enjoyed her occasional conversations with Kyle's spirited assistant.

"Kelly, how are you! It's great to hear from you. I hear business is booming—as always!" Samantha laughed heartily.

"Everything is going great, thanks, Sam. Listen, Kyle called me earlier. Is he in?" Kelly cringed at the quiver she heard in her voice.

"Oh, sure, hang on a second," Samantha said brightly. Kelly waited, tapping her fingers restlessly against her desk. She was just reaching over to hang up when she heard his voice.

"Kelly, sweetheart, how are things?" Kyle's voice was silky smooth and sent a familiar shiver down her spine. She quickly reminded herself of what his voice could be like when things didn't go as planned, things like their relationship for instance. Major tantrums.

"Hi, Kyle, you called earlier?" she answered in a dry tone.

He hesitated, then cleared his throat. "Um, yes, I did. I was wondering if you had decided on whose designs to feature in your fall displays yet."

Kelly rolled her eyes. So predictable! "Actually I have."

"Anyone I might be familiar with?" He chuckled confidently.

"Miller, Karan, Klein. You know, the staples." Kelly smirked as she imagined his chiseled face reddening at the other end.

"No Lenay? What fall display would be complete without one, darling?" Kyle spoke softly, trying to act as if he wasn't at all concerned that his designs had been omitted.

"Mine, Kyle." Kelly was silent for a minute. "I looked over your fall line and I wasn't impressed with any of the designs enough to want to feature them at Taylor-Made." She held the phone away from her ear knowingly and rested her feet up on her desk.

"You've got to be kidding, right? You're saying that you think that Miller has something over my fall designs! Come on, she's an amateur compared to me. Kelly, I really think you're letting your personal feelings get in the way of business here." He snorted loudly into the phone and Kelly backed farther away from the receiver in disgust.

"Get a grip, Kyle. Personal feelings have nothing to do with my decision. Besides, I'm the one that left you, remember?" Kelly hissed.

"Nasty, nasty, Kell!"

"Listen, Kyle, I really don't have the time or the desire to get into this with you. I'm sorry that I didn't decide to use a Lenay, but I don't care for the midcalf length of your designs and the overall slimness isn't attractive on anyone except pencil-thin models. I know my clientele and they wouldn't want something they can't breathe in. That's why I passed on the Lenays for the display; it had absolutely nothing to do with us," Kelly said firmly.

"I think you're making a mistake," he warned her ominously.

"If any of my customers want one of your fall designs, all they have to do is go to the Lenay boutique in each store, no big deal." She sighed wearily. Confrontations with Kyle always left her feeling wiped out. "Well, Kyle, there's no sense in arguing about this. I appreciate your calling, but I have a million other things to deal with today and I don't have the time or the energy to discuss this any further. Take care of yourself and I'm sure that we'll be able to move some of your designs even without them being featured. *Ciao!*" Kelly put the phone down softly and chuckled. She would bet her last pair of shoes Kyle was spitting furiously into his telephone right now. Well, he would just have to learn that Taylor-Made showed no favoritism, even to a designer like Kyle. With a shake of her head she continued sorting through the other phone messages and didn't bother to look up when the door to her office opened.

"Some coffee, sweetie?" Barbara asked from the doorway.

"I would love a cup, thanks." She stifled a yawn as she counted out the number of calls that were important enough to be returned immediately. Barbara placed a steaming coffee cup on her desk and glanced over Kelly's shoulder at her desk calendar.

"Don't forget you have lunch at Contina with the

reporter from the *Times*, okay?" Barbara picked up her notepad and walked around Kelly's desk then sat in one of the cushioned chairs, her pen in hand, ready to start with the day's business.

"I remember. There's no way we can postpone it again, is there?" Kelly knew it would take at least two hours out of her already cramped schedule.

"Absolutely not. The article is set to run next Sunday, Kelly, and we've already rescheduled twice. If I called over there again, they just might take away the Businesswoman of the Year award!"

"All right, all right. It's at twelve-thirty?" she asked, then sipped her coffee.

"Yep, it's with Lisa Roberts, that new hotshot reporter. She probably has gone over everything in your background, so you better be prepared." Barbara smiled sympathetically at Kelly. "Feeling a little over-whelmed?"

"Not that I'm complaining, but it just seems like all I do is waste time on the phone playing politics and doing lunch. Sometimes I wish I could turn back the clock." Kelly rubbed her forehead to ease some of her tension and turned to gaze out the window at the city skyline.

Eight years of hard work had built Taylor-Made into one of the few success stories in the world of fashion retail. Life after West Beverly High had seemed to be filled with mindless wandering—endless shopping sprees, parties at night, and men in expensive cars—until she had decided to buckle down and find herself a career. Kelly smiled as she recalled the hot summer day she had stumbled on the small shop for rent on Rodeo Drive and came up with the idea of an upscale store that carried all the top designer fashions, but had more of a homey feel to it than the normal glitz and glamour of the hundreds of shops that lined the avenue. Brenda and Donna had thought she had finally lost it to invest so much money in such a chancy venture. Now they were two of her best customers . . . even if they didn't always pay their accounts on time! From that one store, Taylor-Made had grown into a five-store chain, with shops in New York, London, and Palm Beach. Success was more than sweet, it was exhausting, Kelly thought as she took another gulp of coffee and turned back to Barbara, who was quietly making notes on her pad. She put her cup down on the desk and picked up a financial report that the accounting department had routed up for her approval.

"These figures need to be reworked, Barb. There's not enough in the advertising budget for the New York store. We're going to move ahead with the TV spots, so it needs to be reflected here. Could you be sure to talk with Dave about it?" She passed the report over and reached for another when the phone rang. "Hold on a second," she said, and picked up the receiver.

"Kelly Taylor," she answered crisply.

"Kell, what's up?" Brenda Walsh sounded extremely cheerful and energetic. Kelly glanced at her watch in confusion.

"Hi, Bren, I'm just trying to sort through this mess of a desk here." Kelly nestled the phone on her shoulder as she wrote on some papers and gave them to Barbara. "What are you doing up so early?"

Brenda laughed. "What do you mean by that? Should I be insulted?"

"Well, since you're not working right now, I would have thought you'd be enjoying every minute, some heavy-duty R and R."

"That's exactly what I was doing, but now I'm getting a little antsy. Did I tell you? I got an audition on Thursday for a new Scorcese film and I've been reading through the script," Brenda explained breathlessly. "But that's something we can talk about later. What I called for is I was wondering if you were free tonight? I thought that maybe you and Donna could come over here for dinner. We haven't gotten together in weeks and Dylan is on the road again, so I figured it would be a great night for some female bonding. What do you say?"

Kelly ran her finger down her calendar and flipped over to the next day's appointments. "I don't know, Bren, we have the fall displays going up in three days and things are kind of crazy here."

"C'mon, Kell. You're always working! It would be good for you to take a break. Pleeease!" Brenda begged.

"Let me see what I can get done this afternoon and I'll call you later, okay? If I can get caught up, I'll be there." Kelly smirked as Barbara nodded at her approvingly from across the desk. "I think Barbara agrees with you that I spend too much time working. She's sitting here nodding at me."

Brenda giggled. "I always did love her! Really, it'll be great and you can tell me what you think of this script. It's really hot and I hear that Gibson may be interested!"

"Sounds good to me already. Any heavy-duty love scenes?" Kelly asked jokingly, knowing the only guy Brenda was attracted to was Dylan.

"Kelly! Listen, I still have to call Donna, so I've got to go. Be here about sixish and I won't take no for an answer. Later!"

Kelly pursed her lips as she listened to the line click. Brenda just couldn't seem to understand the pressure of running a major business like Taylor-Made. She firmly believed that everyone should end their workday at a normal hour. Easy for her to say! Brenda didn't have a regular schedule and often went for months at a time without work.

Perturbed, Kelly pulled a stack of papers toward her and dived in, glancing at her watch occasionally. She and Barbara had managed to weed through three quarters of the paperwork when the receptionist buzzed through and said there was a delivery for her at the front desk.

"Barb, could you see what it is for me? I just want to freshen my makeup a bit before I head out for lunch." Kelly walked quickly into her adjoining bathroom and sat down at the marble topped vanity table. She opened one of the drawers, looking for some blush and lipstick. With a few strokes of the brush and a touch of lipstick, she was finished and had just sprayed some perfume on her wrists when she heard Barb's soft laughter in her office. "What is it, Barb?" she called out.

"I'll let you see it with your own eyes, sweetie," Barb answered with a touch of disbelief in her voice.

Curious, Kelly got up and hurried back into the office then stopped dead in her tracks. The entire side table was covered with dozens of creamy roses in simple cut-glass vases. Barbara stood to the side, sniffing deeply at an arrangement. "Aren't they gorgeous?" she said.

"Where did they come from?" Kelly asked quizzically as she walked over and pulled the card from an arrangement. Her eyes lit up as she read the brief note. Then she looked at Barbara and laughed. "'Now I know why you were voted Businesswoman of the Year. My sincere apologies about this morning. Love, Kyle.' He never changes, that's for sure. He always knew how to get back into my good graces." Kelly snickered and tossed the card into the wastebasket. "I just hope he doesn't think that a couple of hundred dollars' worth of flowers will get me to change my mind about the fall display."

Barbara guffawed. "No, I think he knows you better by now, Kelly. Do you want me to move these?"

"Just leave them there for now. I have to hurry if I'm going to make it on time for lunch. How do I look?" She pirouetted gracefully.

"Gorgeous as always. That suit is to die for, just the right touch. You'll do great." Barbara picked up her stacks of work and headed for the door. "See you around two-thirty, right?"

"I shouldn't be any later. And Barb, if Brenda or Donna calls, just tell them I'll see them later, okay?" Kelly grabbed her briefcase and followed Barbara out the door.

"You bet I will. It's about time you took a night off to have some fun!"

"I know, I know, I work too much! I'll see you in a little while," Kelly said as she started down the hallway, then stopped. "Oh, and Barb, if Kyle calls, tell him I said thanks, but I still won't change my mind."

Barbara's throaty laughter echoed down the staircase as Kelly nodded at several of the sales assistants on the main floor and made her way to the front door. If traffic was as heavy as usual, she had barely enough time to make it to the restaurant before the reporter from the *Times*. With a deep breath she fluffed up her wispy bangs and ran out to jump into her red Jaguar convertible, which was parked directly in front of the store.

As waiters floated smoothly through the room the sounds of clinking china and muffled conversation surrounded the small booth where Kelly and Lisa Roberts sat finishing their coffee.

"So that's the entire story behind Taylor-Made, Lisa," Kelly said, smiling across the table.

"I must say, what you've accomplished in such a short time is quite amazing, Kelly. It's inspiring to see someone like you actually achieve this level of success despite what your critics said at the beginning." Lisa looked at Kelly intently. "What was it . . . oh, yes: 'the party-hearty shopper goes corporate.' Quite a change, wouldn't you say?"

"I definitely don't do the party scene much anymore!" Kelly said with a laugh. "You know it never bothered me what everyone else said when I opened up Taylor-Made. I knew it would work, I just didn't know how big it would be!"

"Kelly, we've managed to cover the entire business angle of your story and I just wanted to ask you a few personal questions, you know, to give our readers a full view of what life is like as the Businesswoman of the Year," Lisa said, stopping the small tape recorder that sat on the table between them. She reached into her bag then replaced the small cassette with a fresh one and hit "record." Kelly watched her anxiously, her body tensing for the next question.

"You're intelligent, successful, beautiful, and available. Is there someone special in your life now?" Lisa smiled at her encouragingly.

Kelly coughed and felt the blood rush to her cheeks. She was always uncomfortable when someone asked about her private life—or lack of one, she thought dryly. "Actually I don't seem to have the time for a relationship these days, Lisa."

"What about Kyle Lenay, the most eligible bachelor in the fashion industry? You two were quite an item for several years," Lisa said as she leaned forward.

"I really don't think that talking about my past relationships will give your readers an inside view of my life, Lisa," Kelly answered evasively. She nervously rubbed her index finger along her bottom lip. If only Kyle would just fade away once and for all, but it seemed as if he kept coming back to haunt her! "I'm sorry; what were you saying?" she said abruptly as she realized Lisa had asked another question.

"I was just wondering if your success got in the way of the relationship? It must have been difficult for a powerful man like Kyle to share the limelight with such a strong woman," Lisa explained. She shifted in her seat, smoothing her skirt, then waited expectantly.

Kelly smirked. Well, Barbara was right again. Lisa had definitely done her homework before this interview. Kelly knew that the only way to deal with the question was honestly and she was sure that Kyle would be furious with her when he saw the article. "Kyle and I had a wonderful relationship for four years. But when Taylor-Made expanded into both London and New York, I didn't have the time to make the relationship work. You're right, it was hard on Kyle. I was constantly traveling and doing heavy promotional appearances and he resented it after a while. I mean, how many men could put up with that life-style?" Kelly chuckled as she remembered one of their explosive arguments when Kyle had insisted he had a better relationship with her answering machine than with her.

"Not many," Lisa agreed sympathetically. "So what's next? Is there anyone else to share in your success?" Kelly shook her head. "Then how about any major plans on the horizon for Taylor-Made? Or more importantly for Kelly Taylor?"

"I'm always looking for new challenges, but right at the moment I'm too occupied getting ready for the fall season." Kelly checked her watch and placed her napkin down on the table. "And I really have to get back to the office and deal with a few things."

"I guess that covers everything anyway. I really appreciate you taking the time to meet with me, Kelly." Lisa packed her tape recorder up and put it in her bag. "You've been a delightful interview and I'm sure you'll be pleased with the finished article. I'll send an advance over to your office later this week." Both women stood up and shook hands warmly, catching the eyes of many diners for their strikingly good looks. One a pale, willowy blonde, the other a fiery redhead. Each woman exuded an air of success.

"Thanks, Lisa, that would be great." Kelly weaved her way through the tables toward the entrance. She nodded at several people she knew and walked out into the bright California sunshine. As they waited for their cars to be brought around, she turned to Lisa. "I do hope you get the chance to stop into Taylor-Made sometime soon. There's a new Asten that would be terrific on you with that gorgeous mop of hair." She eyed Lisa's auburn locks appreciatively.

"Well, it's a little bit above my budget," Lisa said laughingly. "I only allow myself one yearly visit so I don't get into too much debt!"

Kelly nodded. "I know how that feels. That's part of the reason why I started this business—so I could get all my clothes at cost!" Just then the parking valet swung her Jaguar around and jumped out, holding the door open for Kelly. "Thanks again, Lisa," she said as she slid in. With a wide smile she adjusted her rearview mirror and ran her fingers through her hair. As the stereo came on she stepped on the gas and pulled out into the midday traffic, her mind focused on the afternoon business ahead.

"What do you mean, the mums are wilted?" Kelly's voice was shrill as she shouted into the phone at her display manager. "I told Henri to be sure that they were fresh!"

"Kelly, I'm telling you these flowers have been around for aeons. These buds look like rejects from a pet cemetery. You better come down and take a look," André said patiently.

She rubbed her temples. "Give me about five minutes. I'll put in a call to Henri to get his butt over here. Thanks for letting me know, André." She slammed the phone down and yelled for Barbara. "Do you have any aspirin?" she asked when Barb appeared in the doorway.

"Right here." She carried a small glass of water and held her hand out to Kelly. "I had a feeling that the flower problem would put you over the edge."

"You are a doll! I really don't know what I would do without you, thanks." She swallowed the pills, and took a swig of water and grimaced. "How's the rest of the afternoon look?"

"Standing room only, honey. The 'Entertainment Update' crew is here; they're waiting in the reception area," Barbara said, gathering up the remaining papers on Kelly's desk. "Two more flower arrangements were delivered, one from Lisa Roberts and a basket of orchids that is stunning. Don't know who sent those; the card is sealed, and I figured there was a reason." Barb winked at Kelly. "I'll bring them in now. We need to spread these flowers out in here, though, so it doesn't look like a flower shop!" She stopped when she saw Kelly place her head in her hands. "What's the matter, Kell?"

"I completely forgot about the 'Entertainment Update' interview!" Kelly said, looking up at her woefully.

"Nothing to worry about, Kellylou! It's just a short piece on your award. It'll be a breeze!"

"Give me a few minutes to catch my breath, okay, then send them in. And Barb, call Henri and tell him if he doesn't get those mums straightened out immediately, I'm pulling the Taylor-Made account and I mean it this time," Kelly said as she stood up and stretched.

"Consider it done, boss," Barb called out as she saluted and left the office.

Not bad for someone who worked twenty hours a day, Kelly thought as she peered into her mirror searching for some telltale signs of age. She ran a brush through her hair then grabbed a tube of red lipstick and slid it across her lips. With a piece of tissue she blotted away the excess then straightened her blazer. Her feet ached, but there was no time for her to take off her pumps and put her feet up.

With a glance at the full-length mirror on the wall, Kelly walked back into her office. Barbara had spread out the vases of roses and a vine-weaved basket of magenta orchids sat on the low cocktail table in the sitting area, the emerald-green leaves a rich complement to the fragile buds. Kelly reached over and tore the ivory envelope open, wondering who would have sent such a striking arrangement. "Ryan Anderson!"

"Ryan Anderson, you're kidding, right?" Barb walked in and came up behind her, reading over Kelly's shoulder. "I'd give anything to be in your shoes right now, honey. He is the hottest, and I mean hottest, bachelor in this big old country 'tis of thee. How'd you ever hook up with him?"

"I didn't. I don't even know him! Why would Ryan Anderson send me flowers?" she wondered aloud.

"Maybe he saw one of the articles on you and decided to take the leap." Barb fell sideways as Kelly pushed her shoulder.

"I'm serious! I have no idea why he would do this. What should I do, call and thank him?" The thought of it made Kelly's stomach flip. Not only was Ryan drop-dead gorgeous, he was also one of the most powerful entertainment attorneys in the business. What would she say to him?

"I would, if I were you. If you don't want to, though, I'll gladly do it for you," Barbara said.

"Forget about it! I know you, once you get your crimson claws in a man, he's history. I'll call him after the interview. Can you get his number for me?" Barb nodded as Kelly put the card in her top desk drawer. "I guess we better get this show on the road if I'm ever going to get out here tonight. Send the 'EU' people in."

"You got it." Barbara glanced at the orchids wistfully as she walked past. "Kelly, if for some reason, things don't pan out between you and Ryan . . ."

"Would you get out of here! This could be just a friendly gesture. You practically have us married already!" Kelly chuckled as Barb stuck her tongue out then disappeared through the doorway. She could hear voices in the hallway and stood waiting near her desk until Barb returned, trailed by three young men in jeans and sweatshirts and a sharply dressed woman in a scarlet suit with shoulder-length hair as blond as Kelly's own. Her pale face lit up with a toothy smile when her eyes rested on Kelly.

"Diana Hobart, 'Entertainment Update,'" she said as she held out a manicured hand.

"Kelly Taylor."

"I know who you are, Ms. Taylor, as does most of America. I must say this is quite an impressive spread you have here." Diana gazed around the office appreciatively. "Those flowers are simply breathtaking," she said as she pointed at the orchids. Kelly nodded as she caught Barbara's eye and sent a silent warning.

"Where would you like to do this, Ms. Hobart? Is the sitting area all right?" Kelly asked as she walked over to the small burgundy sofa.

"Fine. And call me Diana, please. Do you mind if I call you Kelly? Ms. Taylor sounds too formal and our audience likes things to be open and friendly. You know? Like they're eavesdropping on a conversation between two friends?" Diana smiled and scrunched her perfect nose.

"Of course, Diana." Kelly bit the inside of her cheek to keep from laughing as she watched Barbara raise her nose in the air behind the reporter. "Please, sit down."

"We'll just chat a bit while the boys get everything set up. It shouldn't take long." Diana opened her briefcase and pulled out some notes, then looked up at Kelly. "So tell me, what's it like being the toast of the town? It seems like everywhere I go, everyone is talking about you."

"I wouldn't say I'm the toast of the town exactly. I've just been very fortunate and everyone loves a success story."

The Beverly Hills Beauties—Tori Spelling as Donna Martin, Shannen Doherty as Brenda Walsh, Jennie Garth as Kelly Taylor, and Gabrielle Carteris as Andrea Zuckerman.

Jason Priestley as Brandon Walsh.

Shannen Doherty as Brenda Walsh.

Luke Perry as Dylan McKay.

Jennie Garth as Kelly Taylor.

Ian Ziering as
Steve Sanders.

Tori Spelling as
Donna Martin.

Gabrielle Carteris as
Andrea Zuckerman.

Brian Austin Green as
David Silver.

The Boys of 90210—*Counterclockwise from the top:* Jason Priestley as Brandon Walsh, Luke Perry as Dylan McKay, Ian Ziering as Steve Sanders and Brian Austin Green as David Silver.

"As much as they love a failure? I don't think so. At least not in this town," Diana said dryly.

"Competition is always tough, it's not necessarily just L.A." Kelly stopped and gestured at Barbara. "Barb, could you arrange some coffee and seltzer, please?"

"Of course, be right back."

"That would be great, thanks," Diana said as she glanced down at her notes again. Kelly fidgeted nervously in the silence. Two interviews in one day was cruel and unusual punishment. No one should have to suffer through this.

The camera crew moved swiftly, and within minutes the sitting area had been converted into a miniset. A lighting umbrella was placed to the right of the cocktail table, bouncing the glare of a bright white light into Kelly's eyes.

"Do you think we could move that just a little bit?" Kelly asked, raising her hand as a shield.

"Sure. Hey, David, move that klieg over, will you?" Diana pointed with her pen.

Kelly smiled thankfully. When Barbara came in with the coffee, she reached up to take a cup off the tray. "Thanks, Barb."

Barbara turned to Diana and bent lower to get her attention. "Would you prefer coffee or seltzer, Ms. Hobart?" she asked politely.

"Coffee. Just set it down on the table."

Kelly felt her face tighten at the other woman's impervious tone. "Here, Barb, let me help you." She set the coffee down and turned to the crewmen. "Would you care for something to drink?"

"No, thanks." The three men didn't stop moving as they completed the setup. "Ready to go when you are, Ms. Hobart."

Kelly looked at Barbara pointedly and raised her eyebrows. Ms. Hobart, indeed!

"Ms. Taylor, could you just place this mike on your lapel there?" The crewman held a small black unit toward her.

"Sure." She attached it quickly to her blazer then rested her hands on her lap.

"Ready?" Diana asked sweetly.

"As I'll ever be," Kelly answered.

The cameraman gave a brief count and Diana sat up straight then smiled encouragingly at Kelly.

"Kelly, whatever made you choose fashion retail as a career?"

"I guess it was a natural move for me; I was a shopaholic. I could spend hours and hours hitting the stores with my friends. My mom used to say I was born to shop." She smiled.

"Did you ever think you would be where you are today?"

"Never. I knew I was taking a chance when I started Taylor-Made and a lot of people said I was wasting my time. But something kept me going, and though it seems like it was effortless, it took a lot of hard work and I did have some hard times."

"You mention hard times, could that be referring to the demise of your relationship with Kyle Lenay?" Diana asked firmly.

Kelly frowned. "Yes, that *was* difficult. It's never easy to end a long-term relationship. But actually I was referring to the hard times I experienced with Taylor-Made. At the beginning I was about two days from shutting it down when a friend of mine who's an actress happened to stop in and ordered an entire new wardrobe. With the word of mouth about where she got her clothes, I soon had to hire help to deal with the volume." It was one of the many reasons that Kelly had promised always to stay in touch with Brenda no matter where they ended up. Two days from bankruptcy and she had just waltzed in and charged everything in sight. That was the kind of thing true friends did for each other, as Kelly had learned the hard way.

"Really! But isn't it true that you were brought up in Beverly Hills? I know that most of the lifers around here have some type of trust fund to dip into." Diana's voice was clipped.

"No, it's not true. Sure, some of the people who live in Beverly Hills have money, but not everyone does," Kelly said firmly. People always assumed that she had nothing to lose by going into business. Taylor-Made had taken every single penny she had, and if she had lost it, she would have lost everything. Riled by the tone the interview had taken, Kelly braced herself for the worst. As Barbara hovered in the background she maneuvered carefully through the mine field of questions Diana launched and managed to maintain her cool.

"So now you've managed to capture the Businesswoman of the Year award. How does it feel to be acclaimed as one of the best in the business world?" Diana twiddled her pen as she waited.

"Wonderful. It's an honor to have been chosen and it somehow adds a certain prestige to what I've accomplished with Taylor-Made." Kelly shifted as she felt a rivulet of sweat run down her back. She wanted nothing more than to finish the interview quickly and get away from this viper.

"I'm sure it does. Well, Kelly, I know everyone in the audience wishes you continued success. Without Taylor-Made, who would set the styles of tomorrow?" Diana tittered as Kelly eyed her coolly. "That finishes it, guys. I'll do the open and close at the studio. Kelly, it was a pleasure meeting you, and I just know that no matter what happens with the business, you'll end up on your feet." She gathered her papers quickly as the crew began to pull down the equipment.

"May I ask you a question?" Kelly stood and looked down at the other woman.

"Sure, shoot."

"Are you always so bitchy or do you save it for the days you wear that horrid suit? It really is quite unbecoming. Maybe you should visit with one of my consultants." Kelly turned and started to walk out of the office. "Show Ms. Hobart and her crew out when they're finished, will you, Barb? I have some business to take care of."

"Yes, sir, Ms. Taylor," Barb answered jauntily.

Kelly ducked into an empty office and closed the door. As she leaned against the desk she held her hand to her mouth to hide her laughter. Serves her right, she thought as she picked up the phone and dialed Barbara's extension.

"Barbara Stevens."

"Did you get the number for Ryan?" Kelly spoke softly.

"Uh-huh. Do you want it now? Miss Thing just stalked out. I think you really lit a fire under her with that one." Barb's voice crackled with laughter.

"Someone had to do it! I don't think I could have spent another second with her attitude. And that suit!" Kelly snorted. "Give me the number, I'll call from Donna's office."

"What's it worth to you?"

"Just give me the number!"

"Now don't go getting into a huff about it! It's 971-2549."

"Thanks, I'll see you in a few minutes."

"I'll be waiting with bated breath," Barbara said.

Kelly punched in the numbers and slid on top of the desk as the line began to ring.

"Mr. Anderson's office," a female voice said.

"May I speak with Mr. Anderson, please? This is Kelly Taylor." Kelly blew air on her sweaty palm while she waited to be put through.

"One moment for Mr. Anderson, please," the voice said again.

"Ms. Taylor, what a pleasant surprise!" Ryan had a warm, lilting voice. Kelly smiled in response.

"I just wanted to thank you for the lovely orchids. They have to be the most striking flowers I've ever seen." She thought of the extravagant roses Kyle had sent and how something so simple in its beauty could make his gesture seem so contrived.

"I hoped you would enjoy them. I raise orchids in my greenhouse," Ryan said. "It's been a passion of mine since college and I can never seem to break away from it. Now I have so many different strains, I ran out of space." He chuckled unselfconsciously at his excess.

"I would love to see you—uh, them—I mean your greenhouse, that is," Kelly stammered. She closed her eyes and prayed he didn't notice. Why did she suddenly have to behave like a schoolgirl?

"How about this weekend? I could pick you up at your house on Saturday morning and we could have brunch at my place and then spend the afternoon in the greenhouse." His voice sounded tentative.

"That sounds great! Here, let me give you my address," Kelly said.

"I have it. You forget that since all of those articles are running on you, most of greater L.A. does, too!" He laughed. "How's ten-thirty sound?"

"Perfect. I'll see you then. And Ryan, thanks again for the orchids, they really are beautiful!"

"You haven't seen anything yet. See you Saturday," he said, and hung up.

Kelly dropped the receiver into its cradle and hooted. "I can't believe it. I have a date with Ryan Anderson. Just wait until I tell Brenda and Donna, they're gonna die!" She laughed gleefully and ran down the hallway to her office.

"Barb, I have a date!"

"Well, hallelujah, there is a God in heaven!" Barb answered as she mockingly raised her arms to the ceiling.

"I have a date with Ryan!" Kelly yelled excitedly. She raced to her desk and began to throw papers into her briefcase.

"When?"

"We're going to have brunch tomorrow at his place," she explained hurriedly.

"Kelly, you stepped in something along the way and I want to know what, so I can find me a pile of it and do a two-step!" Barbara stood with her hands on her hips watching Kelly. "I take it we're finished for the day."

"I have got to get over to Brenda's. I can't wait to tell them this one." Kelly giggled. "They'll never believe it!"

"I think they'll believe anything that you tell them," Barb disagreed. "Do you want me to take care of anything before I go?"

"No, just head out and have a great weekend. I'll see you on Monday with all the juicy details." Kelly snapped her briefcase shut and headed for the door. "Did we get the flowers straightened out?"

"Henri was here in a flash when I delivered your message. André said a new truckload was delivered about a half hour ago," Barb said as she pulled down the blinds on the windows. "You just get going and have yourself a crazy weekend, okay?"

"Thanks, Barb, for everything. Triple *mañanas*!" Kelly flew down the staircase and out the front door of the store without stopping. As she opened the door to her Jaguar she felt someone staring at her and turned to see two well-dressed men watching her from the sidewalk. Devilishly she licked her lips and winked at them then jumped into the car and threw the briefcase into the passenger seat. Yes, life was good, she thought as she put the car in gear and pulled away from the curb. And it can only get better!

■   ■   ■

"That is so hot, Kelly! I can really see it," Donna said, gesturing wildly. "It is too perfect. And the name—where did you ever think of it?"

Brandon and Dylan groaned loudly.

"Hey, Kell, how come you don't have a major relationship in your fantasy?" Steve asked abruptly.

Kelly glared at him then said, "Well, running a business would take up too much time and I figure that there will always be a Ryan Anderson around to keep me warm at night, right?" She looked at Brenda and Donna.

"Most definitely! And besides, you did have a long-term relationship with that obnoxious guy!" Brenda pointed out.

Steve snorted. "Yeah, and I wonder who he was based on?"

"Don't flatter yourself, Steve, you don't have an imaginative bone in your body. Don't forget, Kyle was a successful fashion designer, a subject you know nothing about." Kelly sighed and turned back to Donna. "So what were we saying? Oh yeah. We'd have to have a store as big as Magnin's."

"Listen, Steve, why don't you just drop it, man? It was only a goof," Brandon said, nudging Steve's arm as he stared at Kelly. "It's not worth getting pissed off about."

Steve shook his head. "I know. It probably seems real stupid to you, doesn't it? After a year I still let her get to me, can you believe it?"

"Yeah, I can believe it," Dylan said quietly. "Some women just know how to get you right where it hurts." He gazed down at Brenda.

"Don't bring that up again," Brenda said. "Everyone's tired of hearing about how I dumped you!" She touched his cheek affectionately.

David Silver leaned forward and cleared his throat. "Why did you guys split up in the first place, Steve?"

"You know, Silver, sometimes I wonder why I didn't kill you when you wrecked my car," Steve said sourly.

"Hey, I was only asking a question," David said defensively.

"What's the matter?" Donna asked, hearing the tone of David's voice.

"Nothing, nothing at all," Brandon answered quickly. "You girls done playing Barbies or what?" he said with a grin.

"Yes, we're done, Brandon, thank you. Whose turn is it now?" she asked Andrea.

"Actually, Donna, it's Steve's turn." Andrea pursed her lips and watched Steve's face light up.

"Come on, Sanders, let's hear your fantasy," Dylan goaded. "And remember, we're not talking sexual here either." Dylan and Brandon snickered as Steve straightened up eagerly on his blanket.

Kelly shook her head at Donna and tossed a piece of popcorn into the fire. "Fire's getting kind of low, guys."

"I got it," David said as he reached behind Brandon for a couple of small pieces of wood.

"All right, listen up, everybody. The Sandman is about to begin," Brandon shouted out into the still night air.

"Brandon, do you have to make so much noise?" Andrea covered her ears. "We're all right within five feet of you. You don't have to yell."

"Sorry! I was only trying to get everyone's attention," he said as he sat back on the blanket. "What's up with you tonight anyway?"

"Nothing," Andrea said tersely. "Now come on, pay attention."

Brandon took a deep breath. Okay, the great wall of Andrea was in place, that he could see. Well, there was nothing he could do about it right now. Besides, Steve probably had the wildest fantasy of them all and he wouldn't miss it for anything, not even to find out what was bugging Andrea.

Steve

"CASSIE, WHAT A SURPRISE! YOU LOOK FANTAS-
tic!" Steve Sanders pecked the suntanned cheek the
tall, young actress offered him and slid his arm around
Cassie's shoulder, guiding her into his office. "I'm sorry
I never got a chance to give you a call to get together
for that dinner. I hope you aren't too upset with me?"
He looked down at her, his bluish-gray eyes filled with
concern. Cassie Lockburn was not only one of his best
clients, she was also a top-of-the-line classy lady.

"I'm not at all upset with you, Steve. It just under-
scores everything I've always heard about you." She
smiled as she sat down on the overstuffed ivory couch,
her arm gracefully draped across the back of the cush-
ions. "You never mix pleasure with business, right?"

Steve smirked as he poured a cup of coffee and
offered it to her. "Something like that," he said. "I've

found it makes it much easier to deal with life in general. That way the lines never get blurred."

"What a pity!" Cassie murmured, crossing her long legs seductively. Her rust suede miniskirt rode another inch up her firm, muscular thigh. "Maybe I should find a new PR team." She chuckled as she watched Steve blanch. "I'm only teasing, Steve, relax!"

"It's not that I'm not flattered, Cassie. Not at all! If I ever reach the point of wanting a serious relationship, you're definitely the type of woman I would want to be involved with. Seriously," he said as she shook her head at him.

"You truly are a charmer, Steve Sanders! That's what makes you so irresistible, that and those killer eyes," she said admiringly. "But enough of this stuff, let's get down to business. The reason I made this appointment is that I feel as if my public persona needs a major overhaul. I feel as if people have a difficult time realizing that I am not Aliza Hames off the set. It's so crazy: sometimes people come up to me in the grocery store and tell me how I'm such a bitch, I deserve whatever is coming to me!" She absently grabbed her thick mane of red hair and rolled it into a loose bun as she spoke. Her hazel eyes caught the fading afternoon light seeping through the blinds and turned a golden green. Steve coughed and tried to concentrate.

"What you're telling me is that you want people to see the real you, to let them in and see how you live, right?" He took a long sip of his coffee and sat back.

"Exactly," Cassie said firmly.

"You realize that by doing something this aggressive, you're effectively giving up your right to privacy here," Steve admonished.

"What right to privacy?" she asked, then laughed. "My photo's on the cover of every sleazy tabloid in the country. 'Star of "Reservations Required" Doesn't Have to Act to Be Aliza.' If I hear one more time that I'm a prima donna on the set, I'm not only going to scream, I'll murder the person who says it!"

"Cass, come on. Don't take it so seriously! What we can do is come up with a series of interviews, maybe a spread on your beach house or something, and show people the real Cassie Lockburn, away from the set," Steve suggested. "How does that sound?"

"Exactly what I had in mind," she answered, and set her coffee cup down on the table. "Do you think you could pull something together quickly? I know I sound obsessed, but I guess with Shannon going into the first grade and all, I don't want her to have to hear how her mother's such a witch all the time!"

Steve smiled sympathetically. "Ah, so now I see where you're coming from. Has Shannon been affected by all of this, Cassie?"

"She doesn't really say much, but the other day she had some friends over and I overheard their conversation at the pool. She was actually defending me to the other kids, Steve! I was crushed." Cassie's eyes filled with tears. "I always said that my daughter would not be affected by my career and that she would grow up just like an average child. I never thought she would have to defend her own mother. People can be so cruel," she said, and dabbed at her eyes with a tissue she pulled from her bag. "Of course, her father doesn't help the situation. Whenever she spends one of those rare weekends with him, she comes back totally worn down after hearing about what a selfish person I am and how he doesn't get to visit with her that much because of me."

"Shannon is too smart to fall for that," Steve said sincerely as he slid over on the couch and put an arm around Cassie's shoulder. "You're a great mom, and I don't think Shannon would change anything about you." He hugged her and then held her by her shoulders and looked directly in her eyes. "Listen, give me a few days to set some things up, okay? We'll take care of this image problem once and for all."

"Thanks, Steve. Sorry to get so upset on you; it's just a rather sensitive issue with me," Cassie said. She picked up her purse and shoved the ragged tissue in as she stood up and followed him toward the door. "Did you ever think about becoming a therapist?" she asked jokingly.

"Not enough time off," he said as he bent down to kiss her lightly on the forehead. "I'll call you sometime next week, all right? But if something comes up before-hand, just yell. You know where to find me."

Steve smiled widely as he put his hand in the small of her back and escorted her through the empty outer office. Everyone had left for the day, but Steve had waited for Cassie to arrive. "Give my best to Shannon," he called out as she walked toward the elevators. When the doors closed behind her, he turned away smiling. Sure wish you never developed ethics, Steve boy, he thought to himself as walked back into his office and cleared off the table. Women like Cassie were rare, and here he was turning down a wide-open invitation. He must be crazy!

Steve sighed as he deposited the coffee cups in the small office kitchen. He only had forty-five minutes before he had to be at the Peterson dinner. Wandering around the floor, Steve turned off forgotten lights and went back to get his coat and briefcase. He gathered up papers hap-hazardly then glanced at his desk calendar to check the next day's appointments. Back-to-back without a break. He definitely couldn't afford to be out late tonight. Steve stood up and tucked his shirt tightly into his pants then adjusted his brightly colored paisley tie. Tiredly he ran his hand over his face, the twelve-hour golden stubble harsh on his fingers. Fighting a yawn, he closed his brief-case, grabbed his coat, and headed for the elevators. Party time, he thought wearily as he waited.

At least five potential clients would be at this dinner

and it was important for him to be there to make contacts. Steve thought longingly of his bed and wished that he could just grab some takeout Chinese and call it a night. But he knew that the only way to stay on top of the public-relations business was to be out in the public eye at all times. No easy breaks for this kid, he thought sardonically as he entered the darkened garage and automatically pressed the alarm button on his keychain. From its corner niche the midnight-blue Corvette answered. Maybe a relaxing drive in the cool night air with the T top off would give him some energy.

Within minutes Steve was on his way toward Coldwater Canyon, the stereo blasting an old U2 song as he banged his fingers in time against the padded leather steering wheel. The twinkling lights of Los Angeles blurred as he stepped on the gas, the wind whipping past the windshield.

"Steve, thank you for joining us." John Peterson held his hand out and placed the other on Steve's shoulder, leading him toward a small circle of elegantly dressed men. "I believe you know everyone here: Miles Rothberg, Jim Sorens, and Bill Allen. Can I get you something to drink?"

Steve glanced at the other men's hands and smiled at his dark-haired host. "A seltzer would be fine, thanks."

"A seltzer it is," Peterson said smoothly as he headed for a huge wet bar facing the deck.

The view of the valley was spectacular and Steve excused himself from the group and wandered toward the open glass door. Peterson joined him as he stood gazing out at the city lights. "As you requested," Peterson said formally as he handed Steve a crystal glass. "This is one of my favorite spots in the whole house. I often sit out here for hours, just watching the sky and wondering how many lives are unfolding beneath me. It's quite a unique feeling."

"I'm sure it is." Steve smiled and turned to the older man. "How are things on the production end these days, John?"

Peterson Productions had been one of the first accounts he had landed when he opened S.P.R. Over the past five years both companies had grown comparably in size and stature. But things were tight in the film industry and Peterson seemed to be feeling the crunch.

"Tough. It seems like audiences are getting quite particular about what they spend their diminishing entertainment dollar on, and unless you hit right on target, there's no way you can recoup your investment." He slapped Steve casually on the arm. "But I don't want to cry the blues on you all night, Steve. Have you seen anyone else? Tom and Nicole are here with Dustin and Lisa." John motioned for Steve to follow him back into the house. "Lila will kill me if I don't circulate. I'll be back in a while." John smirked and turned away, his attention centered on a stunning, petite dark-haired woman standing near the doorway. "Anna!" he exclaimed as he touched her elbow.

"Steve Sanders, what are you doing here?"

Steve swung around quickly at the sound of the familiar voice, a wide grin on his face. "Courtney, I can't believe it! What are *you* doing here?" He set his glass down and reached for her hand, brushing his lips softly against her knuckles. He had met Courtney Nelson a few years ago when she had first arrived from Oregon searching for her big break. They had become quite friendly, but not as friendly as Steve wanted.

"Uh, uh, uh. You first," she said, giggling. Her dark blue eyes sparkled as she pulled her hand away coyly.

"I've been friends with John for years. Quite a spread, isn't it?" He swung his arm around the cavernous white room.

"A bit intimidating, if you ask me," she said softly. She brushed her hand nervously down the front of her dress. "I feel like I'm playing dress-up or something."

"You look beautiful," he said, letting his eyes roam down the front of her. "Purple is definitely your color."

"I bet you say that to all the girls," she quipped, and swung her long curly brown hair over her shoulder.

"So you didn't answer me. What brings you to the humble abode of John Peterson?" He picked his glass up and casually sipped the seltzer.

"I begged my agent to bring me with him," she whispered. "I know that sounds ridiculous, but I heard that John is developing a new project and I just had to meet him. I thought that a social setting would be better than a formal meeting."

"Ah, now the lights are coming on! Yeah, John did say he had something major in the pipeline." Steve chuckled. "Have you managed to corner him yet?"

"Don't make it sound like that, Steve! It's not like I'm going to force myself on him or anything." Her face turned red and she looked anxiously around the room.

"Well, you could always force yourself on me," Steve suggested, then held his hand up when she glared at him. "Only kidding! Man, you are super-sensitive tonight."

"This is really important to me, Steve. You know I hate playing these power games, but if I'm going to make it in this town, I'll have to play by the rules. You of all people should know that after growing up with a mom who was a major TV actress."

"Yeah, I should, shouldn't I?" Steve gulped his drink. It still made him uneasy when people brought up his mother, the all-American role model for mothers everywhere. Yeah, right. Life in the Sanders household had been far from picture perfect. "Do you want something to drink?"

"A glass of seltzer would be great, thanks." She followed him over to the bar and stood silent while he poured two glasses.

"Here's to you making contact with John," he said as he held his glass up. They touched glasses and sipped, each quietly watching the other people in the room. Agents, actors, and producers socialized effortlessly under the soft, recessed lighting of the Petersons' living room. Everyone seemed friendly and relaxed, enjoying the time spent among friends, but Steve and Courtney both knew the power struggles that simmered beneath the surface of each casual conversation. Sometimes Steve thought it was worse than being the new kid at West Beverly, where one false move made you history. Here, among the movers and shakers of Hollywood, one false move was deadly.

"Did you see Nicole?" Steve asked Courtney.

"When I first came in. She blew me off," Courtney said, and chuckled. "I think she's still bent out of shape about the Golden Globe award."

"She'll get over it," he answered. "I thought you were going to call her and take her to lunch?"

"I tried, but her assistant kept telling me she was unavailable. I can only take so much abuse, Steve, before I say bag it!" Courtney tensed when she saw John look over at them, then turn back to the man he was speaking with. "Who's that John's talking with?"

Steve followed her eyes and smiled. "You're slipping, kiddo! That's Scott Davis, one of the best casting directors around. Must be that he and John are working on something." Steve watched as the two men continued talking, occasionally glancing over at Courtney. "Looks like you caught their eyes, sweetie."

Courtney choked on her seltzer and Steve quickly leaned over to pat her on the back. "I'm okay—"

"A bit uptight, aren't you? Here, take another sip," Steve said as he poured more into her glass from the pitcher on the bar.

"Thanks." She drank quickly and set the glass down. "I don't know why I'm so nervous. It's not like I never had a major role or anything."

"Yeah, but those major parts aren't around much these days and the competition is stiff. Look, Nicole's over there sniffing around now. I think she's got her sights set on John, too."

"Great! Just what I need." Courtney sighed heavily. "You know, this stuff is really starting to get to me. I should have gone to law school or something more secure."

"Ever think of doing some PR work?" Steve asked. "You'd be great at it."

"Thanks, Steve, but don't take me seriously when I get like this. I just can't deal with the cutthroat side of the business. I know that sounds incredibly naive, but I still haven't lost that Oregon side of me yet." She placed her hand on his arm and squeezed gently. "You really are sweet to say that, though."

"I meant it, Courtney, and you're not naive." He looked into her eyes then let his gaze fall to her full lips. Her perfume filled the space between them, teasing him with the spicy scent. Impulsively, he lowered his head and kissed her lips.

"Um, excuse me, Steve." John's voice made Steve pull away abruptly. Abashed, he quickly turned to his friend.

"What is it, John?" he asked.

John smirked at both of them and said, "Sorry to interrupt, but Steve has a phone call. It's your service and they said it was important." He could hardly contain his laughter as he watched Steve and Courtney try to regain their composure. "You can take it in my study if you'd like."

"Thanks, John. Courtney, I'll just be a minute, do you mind waiting?" Steve asked. Spots of light pink appeared on Courtney's cheeks as she shook her head.

"Don't worry about Ms. Nelson, Steve. I've been meaning to discuss a few things with her this evening anyway. This will give us the perfect opportunity," John said as he placed his hand on Courtney's elbow possessively. She squared her shoulders at his touch and Steve could see the anxiety in her eyes.

"I'll just be a minute," he said as he watched them drift away into the crowd. Steve weaved his way through the room and walked down a darkened hallway toward John's book-lined study at the back of the house. The desk light was on and a single phone line blinked impatiently as Steve picked up the receiver. He hit the button and spoke curtly. "Steve Sanders here."

"Mr. Sanders, sorry to interrupt, but we have a message here for you that was keyed in as most urgent." The woman's voice was unsure. "'A crisis at the center; we need your help right away.' They didn't leave a number. I hope we did the right thing in tracking you down at Mr. Peterson's, sir."

Steve's heart skipped. "Of course you did, that's what I pay you for! When did this message come in?" he asked anxiously.

"Over a half hour ago. We had a difficult time finding your itinerary—"

"That's all right, don't worry about it," Steve interrupted. "You did the right thing, thank you." He hung up abruptly and raced down the hallway.

The pace of the party seemed to have picked up and Steve dodged his way through the crowded room, searching for John and Courtney. Finally he spotted them on the deck with Scott Davis and he hurried outside. "John, sorry to interrupt. How are you, Scott?" Steve briefly touched the other man's hand. "Listen, I have an emergency to tend to, so I have to leave. Please give Lila my regrets and tell her I'll make it up to her," Steve said hurriedly. He turned to Courtney and kissed her cheek lightly. "I'll call you later, I promise," he whispered in her ear. She nodded, a tight smile on her lips. "John, I'll call you Monday, okay? Scott, nice seeing you again." With a wave he set out for the deck stairs, knowing it would be easier to leave this way then to try to maneuver out the front door.

A crisis at the center, he thought nervously. That could mean anything. He jogged toward his car and jumped in, the keys already in the ignition, as if he had somehow known he would have to make a quick getaway. The wheels screeched as he slipped into gear and pulled away from the house, throwing up small pieces of gravel behind him as he headed for east L.A.

The large brownstone's beveled windows shone brightly in the darkness as Steve raced down the deserted street, barely stopping as he pulled up to the curb. He grabbed his keys out of the ignition and flew out of the car, racing past the elaborately painted sign that identified the well-maintained building as THE SANDERS CENTER FOR DISADVANTAGED CHILDREN. Taking the stairs two at a time, he hit the top landing at a full run just as the front door opened.

"Mr. Sanders, relax, everything's under control." Jane Cummings held her hand against his heaving chest, gently restraining him. "The crisis is over," she said in her most reassuring voice. As the head psychologist on staff for the center and the mother of six grown children, Jane was an expert in dealing with emergencies. Steve was relieved to see her on duty, but he needed to see for himself that everything was okay.

"What happened?" he asked as he pushed past her and walked briskly into the large foyer. He took several deep breaths and tried to calm his pounding heart as he glanced down the central hallway for any sign of activity. Only the ticking of a mahogany grandfather clock echoed off the silent walls.

"Let's go into my office and I'll explain." She motioned him toward a doorway and he followed obediently. As she slipped behind her desk and sat down Steve paced the floor. "Why don't you sit down and I'll get you a cup of coffee?"

"Just tell me what this all about," Steve ordered. He ran his fingers through his hair as she stared at him coolly. "I'm sorry, Jane, I didn't mean to bite your head off," he said as he lowered himself into a cushioned wingback chair.

"I know. It's upsetting getting that kind of cryptic message. But at the time we didn't know what we were dealing with and I felt it was best that you be notified. I'm sorry we dragged you all the way down here for nothing," she said, and smiled tiredly. "I don't know about you, but I need some caffeine. I'm going to have some tea; would you like to join me?"

"Sure, do you want me to get it?" Steve started to get up, but sat back when Jane breezed past him.

"I'll just be a second. Do you like lemon?"

"No, thanks," he shouted out into the hallway. He listened for her footsteps, but heard nothing. He leaned back and closed his eyes, breathing in deeply. He knew he tended to overreact wherever the kids were concerned, but he couldn't seem to stop himself. Poor Jane always seemed to be the one who had to face him when things went wrong. Steve smirked. I wonder if that was a committee vote, he thought to himself. He sat up straight when he heard her footsteps on the wooden floor.

"Here we are," she said as she handed Steve a steaming mug. She sat down in the chair next to him and sipped cautiously from her cup. "Well, I guess I better get right down to it. All the children had been bathed and dressed by six-thirty and then Lisa had story hour for the older ones before bedtime. Everything was fine until bed check." She paused for a second. "As you know, our routine every night is to go through the nursery first to make sure that all the infants are settled in comfortably. Then we make our way up to the older residents. Michael was with me tonight, and while I checked on the five three-year-olds we have in-house, he took over the fours. Apparently, he helped Bobby Wilkins to the bathroom and when he came back, he realized that Jake Ramiro was missing."

"Jake was missing!" Steve sputtered, nearly spilling his tea.

"Nothing to get upset about, Mr. Sanders, I'll explain." She blew across the top of her cup and then took another drink. "Everyone is aware of the problems Jake's experienced in adjusting to life here at the center. So after checking the bathrooms and under the beds in the four-year-old bedroom, our first thought was that he must have run away."

Steve drew his breath in sharply. A little boy, four years old, wandering around the deadly streets of east Los Angeles at night: a true nightmare. He leaned toward Jane anxiously.

"I sent five of the staff members out into the neighborhood to see if they could find Jake or anyone that might have seen him." Jane's face was expressionless as Steve nodded approvingly. "Then Michael, Lisa, and I searched the house from top to bottom with the help of some of the older children. We didn't want to get the younger ones upset, so we told them we were searching for a lost key. They didn't seem to be concerned, thankfully. I would have hated to have gotten them all upset, too."

"So what happened, Jane? Where was he?" Steve asked impatiently.

"I'm getting to that. When the interior search proved unsuccessful, we waited for the others to return from their canvass of the neighborhood. At that point, when we still had no idea of where Jake could be, I called the police. While I waited for a squad car to arrive

I tried to think of all the places that meant something special to Jake, or of the most important possessions he has. Since he's been with us, I've tried to do a complete work-up on his case to help facilitate his adaptation here. After glancing through his file, I went up to check his bed, to see if his bear and blanket were there. I truly felt that if they were, he hadn't left the house, or if he had left, it wasn't willingly. That's when I saw that his bear was on his pillow, but the blanket was missing."

"He'd never leave his bear behind!" Steve said firmly. Since Jake had been sent to the center three months ago, Steve had made it a personal mission to spend many weekends playing with the slight, tow-headed boy. Jake never smiled. It was as if he were afraid to be happy. It tore at Steve every time he saw Jake dragging his faded bear and tattered blanket with him as though they were the only dependable things left in his young life.

"Yes, you're right, he wouldn't. So I asked everyone to search again, and that was when Karen, the housekeeping aide, remembered. Apparently she had made a deal with Jake after lunch that if he would let her borrow his blanket for a few hours, she would bring it back all nice and clean. Jake was suspicious, but the blanket smelled awful and he gave it to her after she promised he'd have it by bedtime. With the craziness of bath time, she totally forgot about it, but apparently Jake didn't. Everyone rushed down to the laundry room and there was Jake, sound asleep in a wicker basket with his blanket wrapped around him." Jane laughed with relief.

"Where is he now?" Steve asked.

"Back in bed with both his bear and his newly cleaned blanket," Jane said. "I thought we'd have a problem getting him to bed with all the ruckus, but he seemed totally oblivious to everything. By that point we had the police here, too, so you can imagine how crazy everything was. I had Michael call your service after the first house search because I knew you'd want to be here in case something was really wrong. I'm sorry I interrupted your evening, but I must say I'm happy that everything ended up okay."

"Don't worry about it, Jane. I want you to call me when there are problems," Steve assured her. With the financial backing of his parents and several wealthy friends, Steve had purchased the condemned brownstone and had painstakingly restored it before founding the Sanders Center. Four years and one hundred twelve children later, they were bursting at the seams and Steve loved every minute of it. Whenever he could spare the time, he helped out with the daily running of the center. It gave him joy to give these kids a fighting chance in the world. Steve had learned himself the hard way just how important that was when you were growing up. "Do you think I should just pop up and see if he's okay?"

"I think he's probably sound asleep by now, but if you want to, go ahead." Jane grinned at him as she stood up. "He is special, isn't he?"

"Yeah, he is. He reminds me of someone I used to know," Steve said as he walked out into the hallway with her.

"Really? A friend?" she asked, puzzled.

"You could say that," he answered as he headed for the huge staircase. "I'll stop in on my way out. Hey, Jane," he said from the bottom step, "thanks for everything. I'm glad you were here."

She nodded and said, "No—thank you, Mr. Sanders, for caring about these children. I'll see you in a bit." She disappeared through the swinging door that led into the kitchen.

Steve crept up the stairs quietly, trying not to awaken any of the children. At the second floor landing he turned down the dimly lit hallway, tiptoeing toward a partially closed door. The soft sounds of snoring wafted across the threshold and Steve peered into the darkness. As he pushed the door open a shaft of light widened across the room and Steve saw a pair of blue eyes watching him intently. Smiling, he slipped soundlessly across the floor and sat down on the bed beside the small child.

"Hey, buddy, what are you doing still awake?" Steve whispered.

"I dunno," Jake whispered back, then stuck his thumb in his mouth.

"I hear you went on a little adventure, huh?" Steve tickled the boy's belly lightly, trying to make Jake smile. "What, are you going to be an explorer when you grow up or what?"

"I dunno," Jake mumbled. His eyes were wide as they watched Steve, the long blond lashes almost invisible.

"I don't know," he mimicked, and tousled Jake's curly mop. "What do you know?"

"I found my blanket," Jake announced proudly, and held it up so Steve could see with his own eyes.

"So I hear! Didn't you think Karen would bring it back to you?"

"She forgot and it was bedtime," he answered matter-of-factly. "Boo Bear can't sleep without my blanket." He jammed his thumb back in his mouth and his eyelids drifted downward. Steve sat silently watching, then pulled the bedcovers up snugly around Jake's chest.

"Sleep tight, Jake," he said softly. "Maybe we can go catch a ballgame tomorrow or something. Just you and me." He stood up quietly and started for the door.

"Okay, we go to a ballgame. Just you and me, buddy," Jake said, smiling around his puckered thumb as his eyes slowly closed.

Steve grinned in the darkness, watching the little boy as his breathing steadied into the soft rhythm of sleep. Yeah, Jake did remind him of someone he used to know a long time ago—himself.

■ ■ ■

"Yo, Steve, man! I never knew you actually had a heart buried underneath all that muscle, what gives?" Brandon looked at his friend in astonishment.

"Hey, what can I tell you, I'm a nineties kind of guy— tough on the outside, as soft as a baby's behind inside," Steve said good-naturedly as he hit Brandon in the arm.

"Really, Sanders, that whole life-style could be deadly to that mighty macho image you've been building," Dylan commented. "I mean, actually spending time helping little kids and all isn't part of the lesson plan for 'How to Pick Up Chicks 101.' You know what I'm saying?"

"Hey, guys, lighten up, will you? It's just that after everything I went through with my mom and finding out I was adopted, I know how tough it is to be a kid growing up on your own. You need all the help you can get. I just hope that someday I'll really be able to do something like that." Steve rubbed his hands together then opened them wide, holding his palms out to the warmth of the fire.

"But then how come you weren't settled down with your own family?" Donna asked loudly, puzzled. "If I were you, after everything you went through, that would be one of the first things I did."

"Ah, but see, I'm a firm believer that the best things come to those who wait," Steve explained, his eyes fixed on Kelly.

Kelly squirmed on her blanket. She dipped her finger in the sand and focused her attention on drawing aimless circles over and over.

Steve smirked. "Besides, between my high-profile job and all the kids at the center, I really won't have time for a relationship," he said. "But I'm sure that there will be no shortage of lovely ladies anxious to keep me warm at night."

Brandon snickered as he watched David's face

light up with admiration. "C'mon, Silver, he's not serious. Remember this is only a game."

"But Brandon, just think of how women would react to a man like that, it would be incredible! It's the perfect hit," David exclaimed. "It's like what my dad used to do, going up to a girl in the grocery store and asking her how to cook something. They just can't resist giving you advice and *wham!* Before you know it, she's inviting you for dinner at her place. A bunch of little kids would be major heartstrings!" He slapped his hands together enthusiastically.

"Only in his dreams," Kelly interrupted as she raised her soda can to Steve in a mock toast.

"What's the matter, Kell, jealous?"

"Get over it, Steve, will you? You've got nothing I would be jealous over. Believe me, I know," she snapped impatiently.

"Hey, guys! Cool it!" Andrea exclaimed. "Can't you just forget about the past and have a good time? It's getting pretty old listening to the two of you throw daggers at each other all the time."

"Yeah, Andrea's right, knock it off," Brandon echoed. "This is supposed to be a party, remember? P-a-r-t-y. You know, hang out, have a few laughs, that kind of thing."

"Brandon's right, Steve," Donna said. "Besides, everyone here knows that you're one big hunk of manly manhood!" She cracked up as Brenda buried her face in Dylan's shirt, trying not to laugh.

Steve shot her a dirty look. "Very funny, Donna. Sounds like you went to the same charm school as Kelly."

"No, I was born with it," she quipped.

Steve's face flushed and he stuck his chin out belligerently. But he was willing to give in this time. "Okay, enough! What do you say we call it a truce for the night?"

Kelly and Donna looked at each other questioningly then turned back to Steve and nodded. "No more sarcastic remarks?"

"No more sarcastic remarks," he agreed.

"Will wonders never cease," Andrea said dryly. "Could we continue with this or should we call it a night?"

"No way! If I had to do it, everyone has to do it. That's the deal, remember?" Brandon protested.

"Of course I remember, Brandon; I just thought that maybe everyone was getting a little tired of listening—"

"We're having a ball, aren't we, Dylan?" Brenda looked up at her boyfriend with a playful smile on her face.

"I wouldn't miss this for the world," he said.

"Well, that settles it. I guess it's my turn for the spotlight, huh?" David said, looking around at his friends.

"Actually it's mine," Donna answered with a giggle. Everyone looked at her expectantly, but she sat on the blanket motionless. "What?"

"What do you want, a parade? Come on, Donna, just dive in, it's easy," Brandon said teasingly. "Just forget we're all here, staring at you. You have to close your eyes and just picture the ultimate life you would want. It's a piece of cake."

"Okay," she said obediently as she closed her eyes. "Like this?"

"Exactly," he answered, his tone encouraging. Steve tittered and Brandon pointed a menacing finger at him to keep quiet.

Donna was oblivious to everyone around her. With her head slanted up to the night sky and her eyes firmly shut, she was the picture of total concentration. "I've got it," she shrieked as her eyes flew open. She shuffled closer toward the firelight, her hands moving faster than her mouth. "You know how I do well with numbers and everything. . . ."

Brenda glanced over at her brother. Brandon just knew how to do things like that, give someone a little push when they needed it. When she caught his eye, she winked at him and gave him a thumbs-up. He grinned back then held a finger to his lips and pointed at Donna.

Donna

"KELLY, I NEED YOU TO SIGN OFF ON THOSE figures today," Donna yelled into the phone. "How are you going to do that if you're still in Paris?"

"Don't worry about it, I'll grab the Concorde and be in the office this afternoon, all right?" Kelly's voice was amazingly upbeat as soft strains of classical music played in the background.

"Exactly where are you anyway?" Donna asked. What was supposed to have been only a three-day trip to France to oversee the buying for the new store had turned into a week and a half, and Donna was more than suspicious.

"Paris, of course," Kelly answered evasively, then giggled. The line grew muffled, as if a hand had been placed over the receiver, but Donna could hear a lively exchange of voices.

"Kelly, listen to me. If you want to play, that's fine, but you should at least be up front with me about it. We're trying to run a business, remember? Kelly? Kelly, what are you doing?" she asked, exasperated. Distinct kissing noises came over the phone line, followed by a deep voice, murmuring softly in French. Donna's face burned. "Call me when Don Juan leaves," she said hotly as she slammed the phone down on her desk, sending a pile of papers sailing through the air.

The quarter close was only three days away and here Kelly was playing tiptoe through the tulips with some Frenchman. Donna shook her head. She should have known better than to let her go to Paris in the spring by herself! Now it was up to Donna to get everything together and go over all of the reports by Friday. It wasn't the first time she'd had to pinch-hit for Kelly, and usually Donna enjoyed the added responsibility. But things were moving full speed at Taylor-Made and twenty-four hours just wasn't enough time for Donna to deal with all the issues that came her way. Being chief financial officer of a large company wasn't easy; she had learned that as soon as she took the job with Kelly after graduation. Within three years she had managed to double Taylor-Made's operating profit and had helped to devise the expansion program into three other major markets. Paris was their next opening and that was the reason Kelly was there. Not to see if what they said about Paris in the spring was really true. Frowning, Donna hit the intercom button. "Mary, could you pull together New York's sales projections for me please?"

"Of course, I'll be with you in a few minutes," her secretary answered crisply.

"Thanks," Donna said, and collapsed in her chair, holding her head in her hands. Looks like another marathon, she thought to herself as she sighed deeply. Fine, there was nothing she enjoyed more than a challenge. She swung her long blond hair back, put on her tortoiseshell glasses, and adjusted the reading light. Picking up a well-chewed pencil, she began to make corrections on the first pass of the quarterly report and soon lost track of time. She didn't stop when her secretary brought in the figures she had requested.

"Here's the projections, Donna. Did you need anything else?" Mary stood in front of the desk. Her short gray hair and British accent added a maternal air to her appearance, which was deceiving. Fiercely loyal to both Taylor-Made and Donna, Mary was a matron of steel when it came to running the office. She knew a major deadline was looming and was prepared to roll up her sleeves and pitch in; Donna only had to say the word.

"No, thanks." Donna answered, pushing her glasses up on her nose.

"You still don't want to be disturbed with calls, correct?" Mary said as she opened the door.

"Mary, if I had to spend any time on the phone right now, we'd never get this done." Donna groaned as she waved her arm over the stacks of papers covering her desk. "But if Kelly should call in, I definitely want to speak with her!"

Mary arched her eyebrows and formed a small circle with her mouth. "I take it we are on the outs with Ms. Taylor?"

"Outs isn't the word for what I am with Kelly right now," Donna said ominously. "If she calls in, she's mine. Be sure to tell Barb, too."

Mary laughed as she left the office, leaving Donna to focus on the figures in front of her.

"I'm telling you, Brenda, she's met some gigolo or something and she's disappeared! I've been on the phone all morning to the Paris office trying to track her down and no one knows where she is." Donna reached for her water glass and took a sip. "This is exactly what I told her I wouldn't put up with if we worked together. She's left me carrying the load here while she goes and plays Romeo and Juliet."

Brenda listened wide-eyed then started to giggle. "You mean you could actually hear them?" Other diners in the small dimly lit restaurant turned to stare at their corner booth as her laughter started to build.

"Shhh! It's bad enough now, you don't have to broadcast it to half of Los Angeles," Donna chided. Nervously she glanced around then picked up her fork, twisting the pasta on her plate. "I know you think it's humorous, but I'm a little worried, Brenda. I mean, this guy could be anybody!"

"You're right! And knowing Kelly, he's really hot!" Brenda laughed again then wiped the smile off her face when she saw Donna's frown. "All right, I'll be serious about it. Yes, it's unprofessional of Kelly to do something like this, but you would probably do the same thing if you were in her shoes." She hesitated, thinking hard for a second. "Okay, maybe you wouldn't. But Donna, Kelly is a big girl, she can take care of herself. I don't think you should worry about her. She'll show up sooner or later."

"And what am I supposed to do, just take care of everything like always? Give me a break, Brenda. This is totally unfair of Kelly to dump on me," Donna said, her voice rising.

"But that's what she hired you for, remember?" Brenda placed her hand on Donna's and looked her squarely in the eye. "You knew it was going to be tough to work together, but you said you could handle it. After Wharton, you said you could handle Attila the Hun if you had to. And look at all you've accomplished there."

Donna groaned loudly and shook her head. "I know all of that, Bren, that's not what I'm talking about!"

"What *are* you talking about?" Brenda asked firmly. With a flourish she wiped her lips then placed the checkered napkin on the side of her plate.

Donna sat motionless, looking down at her untouched food. Tentatively she glanced up at her friend, not sure of how to answer. "I don't know . . . I mean, it's not like I haven't done any quarterlies without Kelly's input before. I don't know why I'm reacting this way. Isn't it weird?"

"No, it isn't weird at all. You know what I think this is all about?" Brenda lowered her voice and glanced behind her to be sure no one was listening. "I think you wish you were the one playing Romeo and Juliet."

Donna's face flushed bright red and she started to protest.

"Wait a second. Before you say anything, just let me finish." After Donna agreed, Brenda continued. "Ever since you've been back in Beverly Hills, all you do is work. Your entire life revolves around Taylor-Made. That's great—up to a point. It got you where you are now, and between you and Kelly, you've managed to build a name for the business. But what about Donna? You never get out anymore. I had to practically beg you to meet me for lunch today! What I'm saying is that you need a life . . . no, not a life, you need a date!"

"Brenda! I date! You make me sound like a spinster who's locked away in a tower somewhere. Lighten up a bit, will you?" She crinkled her brow disdainfully.

"When's the last time you went out on a date? Tell me," Brenda demanded, her blue eyes sparkling. She reached across the settee and rummaged through her handbag, pulling out a tube of lipstick with a small compact. "Well?" she said as she painted her lips cinnamon red.

"Uh, probably New Year's Eve with that banker I was seeing for a bit in the winter." Donna shrugged nonchalantly at Brenda. "It wasn't any big deal."

"So who would be?" Brenda asked as she shut the compact with a sharp snap. "Are you interested in anyone?"

"No, not exactly." She pushed her plate aside then leaned forward. "Actually I've been talking a lot with this guy I met through one of the designers. He's some kind of a hotshot investor. All I know is he's gorgeous!" Donna giggled.

"Then what are you waiting for? Go after him," Brenda coaxed.

"I don't know. I do have to return his call; he called yesterday after I had tried to find out where Kelly was. I was so pissed I told Mary to hold all my calls. A slight overreaction to the situation, wouldn't you say?"

"Call him. See what he wants, I put money on it you'll be surprised," Brenda suggested with a leer. "You go out and have some fun; I guarantee you, Kelly's little fling won't bother you anymore."

Donna turned as the waiter approached the table. "Ladies, would you care for something else?" he asked, and rubbed his hands together. "How about some ricotta cheesecake, fresh strawberries. Dat sound good?"

The two women stared at him, unsure, then caught each other's eyes. "Dat sounds wonderful, we'll take it," they both answered, and then broke into giggles as he scurried away.

"How did you find this place?" Brenda asked as she looked around at their drab surroundings. Chianti bottles wrapped in straw sat on each table, their rainbow-colored wax drippings telling the tale of their lengthy existence. The room was drowning in crimson, from the checked tablecloths and linens to the dusty curtains at the front windows. The only relief came from the worn, wooden tables and booths lining the walls.

"It's close to work. . . ." Donna started to explain then stopped. "You know, Brenda, you're right. I need a life. Everything I do lately centers around Taylor-Made. Look at me!" She tapped her hand to her forehead in disgust.

"Now you're talking!" Brenda agreed. "Get out and have a good time. It'll be the best thing for you. Oh, look—here comes the cheesecake. You're going to have to wheel me out of here after this!" She smiled sweetly at the waiter as he placed the large hunk of cheesecake surrounded by a small mountain of strawberries in the middle of their table. Eagerly she picked up one of the forks and said, "Look at it this way, Donna. You only live once, so you better enjoy it!" Brenda carved off a large piece and shoved it into her mouth, uttering small sounds of approval as she chewed. "This is heaven, isn't it?" she asked as she reached over for another forkful. Donna laughed, then grabbed the other fork and dug in.

"She still hasn't called," Donna said with disbelief as she dropped her purse on the side table and slipped out of her jacket. "I can't believe her!"

Mary shook her head and crossed the room to Donna's desk, picking up papers that Donna had made corrections on. "Barbara spoke with her briefly. She said that she was going to take a little vacation in the south and she'd be back in the office on Monday."

"Well, that's just great. I take it she forgot about the quarterly close, right?" Donna looked at Mary's face and realized her voice had an edge to it. "I'm sorry, Mar, I didn't mean to take it out on you. It's just that sometimes I wonder what I'm doing working for Kelly. This is completely irresponsible! She's probably on a beach somewhere on the Riviera with this guy, and here I am, stuck in smog-filled Los Angeles, up to my eyeballs in reports." Donna stood at the window and stared off at the horizon. The streets were filled with lines of cars and people shuffled on the crowded sidewalks below, rushing to their destinations. It seemed so cold and impersonal to her. Her entire life seemed cold and impersonal. Brenda was right, she needed to get out. With a heavy sigh she turned back to her secretary. "I think I need a vacation myself," she said with a tired grin.

"You should. You definitely deserve it," Mary said, her concern evident in her face.

"You must have been talking with Brenda," Donna answered halfheartedly.

"What?"

"Never mind, it was nothing. Don't worry about me, Mary. I'll be fine, I promise. What I need for you to do for me right now more than anything is get me the revised pages as soon as possible." Donna sat down and picked up her glasses from the desk as Mary walked toward the door. "Hey, Mary, did Jonathan Rosenfield call again?"

Mary stopped with her hand on the doorknob. "Funny you should ask. His office called while you were out to lunch. There's a message in your pile there," she explained, pointing to the small stack of pink slips on Donna's desk. "He didn't leave a message, just wants you to call him."

Donna's face lit up as she flipped through the small pieces of paper. "Here it is, thanks." She put her glasses on and reached for the phone as the door closed behind Mary. Her throat felt dry as the line started to ring.

"Powell and Rosenfield, may I help you?"

"Mr. Rosenfield's office, please."

"May I ask who's calling?" The woman's tone was distant and protective.

"It's Donna Martin returning his call," she said politely. She couldn't understand why it was so difficult to get through to senior management in the corporate world these days. To Donna, all the power plays were a major waste of time.

"Mr. Rosenfield's office."

Donna rolled her eyes and sighed. "Jonathan Rosenfield, please. It's Donna Martin returning his call." She was sure that the operator had already identified her, but it was part of the game and she had to play it if she was going to get through.

"One moment, please, Ms. Martin," the woman said, and Donna listened to the silence. She read through another report while she waited, losing herself in the familiar world of figures. She jumped when her concentration was broken by his voice.

"Donna, thanks for calling me back. How are you?" Jonathan had a heavy New York accent that made her feel as if she were somehow flirting with danger just by talking to him.

"I'm fine. A bit overwhelmed at the moment, trying to get a close report together. How about you? Have you seen Solly lately?" she asked, realizing it had been weeks since she had spoken with the young designer herself.

"Just last week as a matter of fact. He was going to Mexico with a friend before the season started. He looked great," Jonathan said, and chuckled. "Listen, I was wondering if you had any nights free this week? Maybe we could get together for dinner or something?"

"Um, let me see," Donna answered evasively. She ran the tip of a pencil along her appointment book. "This week is kind of crazy for me with the quarter ending. . . ."

"Come on, it'll do you some good to take a break from the books. How about tomorrow night? We could have an early dinner so that you aren't exhausted. I know this great little French place just past West Pico." He spoke hurriedly, as if he were afraid Donna would cut him off.

"Well, I don't know," she said, grinning. She

couldn't believe she was actually toying with him like this. Kelly's habits must be rubbing off, she thought with a grimace. "Actually, Jonathan, that sounds like a wonderful idea."

"Great, how about I pick you up at eight at your place? You'll have to give me directions, though." Donna could hear papers shuffling. "Okay, shoot."

As she gave him directions to her small house high up in the hills, she twisted her blond hair nervously, thinking about what she should wear. Something sexy, but not too sexy. She didn't want Jonathan to get the wrong idea—but she did want him to be interested. As he read back what he had written down her mind wandered through her overcrowded closet, visualizing possibilities. "Perfect," she said as he finished. "So I'll see you at eight then?"

"If I have any problems, I'll give you a call," Jonathan said cheerfully. "I'm really looking forward to this, Donna."

She smiled into the phone then said shyly, "Me too," and hung up. This definitely called for a quick sweep through the store to see if there was something that caught her eye. Donna glanced at her watch as she reached up to turn off the reading lamp. If she hurried, she had at least two hours to find the perfect outfit before the store closed. Grabbing her purse, she scooted out the door, calling out to Mary that she'd be back in a few hours. Brenda was right, she thought as she rushed down the stairs to the main floor, a night out is exactly what I need! For the first time in a week Kelly's absence had slipped to the back of her mind.

"Good afternoon, Donna," the young sales assistant said as Donna approached. She finished rearranging a choker display on the counter and stood up straight, towering over Donna.

"Hi, Bree, how's the day been?" Donna automatically slipped back into her business mode and gazed around the busy sales floor.

"Hectic. But I'm not complaining," Bree added quickly. She touched her hand to the slick French twist that held her long brown hair in place.

"Let's hope it stays this busy!" Donna smiled and eyed at Bree's black minidress appreciatively. "Listen, Bree, I need to find something to wear for a date tomorrow. That dress looks fantastic on you, but I was thinking of something a little more demure. Do you think you could help me? I know it's kind of crazy down here right now."

Bree waved her hand. "Don't worry about it! I'd love to help. But first you have to tell me who he is and where you're going so I can get some ideas rolling."

"He's the head of an investment firm, very successful and very attractive," Donna explained as they walked toward one of the boutique areas. "This is our first date and I have to look spectacular."

"I guarantee you, Donna, after we're finished, he won't stand a chance," Bree assured her. "What size are you, about a six?" Donna nodded as they headed toward a large display of colorful dresses. "Where are you going?"

"Dinner at some French restaurant," she answered as she pawed through a rack of dresses.

"And then what?" Bree asked suggestively.

Donna looked up, embarrassed. She opened her mouth to berate Bree when she saw the twinkle in the other woman's eye. She definitely did need to get out and have some fun if something as little as that comment could upset her. She pulled out a black off-the-shoulder shift and held it up to her chest. "What do you think?"

"Too much skin," Bree answered, shaking her head.

Donna turned to a mirror nearby. "Yeah, you're

right, too much skin." She put the dress back on the rack. "Any suggestions?"

"Just what I was hoping you'd say," Bree said with a grin, curling her finger at Donna. "Follow me. I've got just the dress for you."

The steam rising from the water fogged up the entire bathroom, but Donna didn't notice as she sank deeper into the warm, white suds. Eight straight hours of paperwork and she had finally managed to finish the report at five. Now the weekend was hers to enjoy, starting with her date with Jonathan. She raised her left leg and rubbed the silky bubbles into her skin. Her eyes grew heavy as the heat drained the stress from her body. She was on the edge of sleep when the ringing of the phone startled her.

"Oh, great," Donna mumbled as she dragged herself out of the tub, grabbing one of her huge bathtowels. Rushing into her bedroom, she picked up the receiver. "Hello?"

"Donna, hey, it's Jonathan. Did I interrupt you?"

She clutched at the top of the towel with one hand, water dripping down the back of her neck. "Of course not, what's up?"

"Well, I have a little problem with tonight," he said quickly. Then his voice faded away.

"Jonathan? Are you there?" Donna asked, a frown on her face. So much for her evening out!

"Sorry, I lost you for a minute. These car phones aren't any good in the hills," he said jokingly. "So is it okay with you then?"

"Is what okay?" Donna felt herself growing irritated.

"If I pick you up in about twenty minutes?"

A jolt of energy surged through her body as her eyes flitted across the room to the clock. "Twenty minutes?" she said as she dropped the towel and ran into the closet, the cordless phone tucked tight to her shoulder. "No problem, I'll be waiting." She grabbed the purple-and-gold dress bag off the rack and squatted down to the rows of shoes lining the floor.

"Great, see you then," he answered, and the line died.

"Twenty minutes!" Donna screeched as she picked up a pair of black slingbacks and raced back into the bedroom. She pulled on her stockings and slip, then slid the bright red dress over her head. Squirming, she managed to reach behind her, pulling the zipper up to the top. Slipping her shoes on, she tottered over to the closet and checked her appearance in the full-length mirror.

The red dress clung softly to her curves and ended a few inches above her knees, making her legs seem even longer. The full-length, tapered sleeves flattered the low-cut neckline which came to a point above Donna's chest. It was simple, yet classic, with just the right touch of sexiness that she was sure Jonathan would have to notice.

She scurried over to her makeup table and sat down, running a brush through her hair vigorously. With a few quick spurts of hairspray, she had arranged her golden mane so that it swept off her forehead and down the side of her face. A little bit of makeup and some perfume then she'd be ready. Grabbing some mascara, she held the wand to her eyelash when the doorbell rang. Groaning, Donna glanced at the clock and saw that it had to be him. This was not how she had planned the night to begin, she thought as she walked to the front door.

"Hey, come on in," she said warmly as she held the door open wide. Jonathan stood on the front step in a black trench coat, his dark hair shining in the soft rain. "I'm not quite ready yet, so why don't you have a seat?" Donna led him into her small living room. "Would you like some coffee or something? A towel maybe?" She giggled nervously.

"No, thanks, I think I'll just drip-dry," he quipped. "But I wouldn't mind that coffee you mentioned." He slipped out of his coat and laid it over the back of the couch. "Nice place."

"Thanks. Uh, I'll be right back, make yourself at home," she stammered as she hurried down the hallway.

Rushing around the kitchen, Donna tried to calm her nerves. It wasn't like she didn't know Jonathan, she had met him several times before. Always with the security of other people around, though, she thought to herself as she waited for the water to boil. The double-breasted gray suit he wore fit snugly and her face grew heated as she pictured what he would look like in a pair of faded jeans. She spilled the hot water as she poured it through the coffee filter. This was ridiculous, she was acting like a schoolgirl! With a deep breath she gathered up the sugar and cream then set them on a small serving tray and walked back into the living room.

"Here you are," Donna said cheerfully as she set the tray down on the coffee table. Jonathan stood looking at the framed pictures on her wall.

"Who's this?" he asked, pointing to a color photo taken on a beach.

"Oh, it's Kelly, me, and another friend when we were in high school." She walked over and stood beside him. "Brenda and I are really close. She moved to Beverly Hills when we were juniors and we've been friends ever since."

"She's pretty," he said as he stared at the photo. Donna glanced at him, troubled by his tone. He turned and smiled then placed his hand on her arm. "But nothing compared to you."

The warmth of his voice flowed over her and she looked away. "I'll be ready in a few minutes, promise."

"Don't take too long," he called after her. "Our reservation is for seven."

Closing the bedroom door, she leaned her forehead against the wood and tried to calm her nerves. Purposefully she sat down and applied her make up then dabbed perfume on the inside of her wrists. With a final touch of lipstick she closed her purse and picked her jacket up off the bed. Here goes, she thought as she turned off the light behind her.

"You look beautiful," Jonathan said, standing as she entered the room.

"Thank you, so do you," she answered, then blushed. "I mean, you look terrific."

He chuckled softly and came over to her, taking the jacket from her hands and holding it open. "Allow me."

She slipped her arms in quickly, her heart pounding so loud she was afraid he would hear. For one moment she felt him lean forward, his breath close to her ear. She moved away and headed for the door. "Looks like it finally stopped raining," she said brightly as she stepped onto the walkway. "You can just close that behind you."

Jonathan pulled the door shut tight and then hurried to open the passenger door to his car. Donna balked when she saw that it was a Porsche, but somehow she managed to slide into the low seat gracefully, her long legs tucked tightly beneath the dashboard. She pulled her dress down as far as possible and sat back as Jonathan climbed in. With a quick turn of the ignition they backed out of the driveway and headed into the darkness for the bright lights of downtown Los Angeles.

Donna sat quietly, listening to the soft music on the stereo and watching the hills fly by. She glanced at Jonathan out of the corner of her eye as he drove. His long, dark hair swept over his collar, adding a sense of daring to his looks. With his high cheekbones and heavily lashed eyes, there was something almost too pretty about him. Donna shifted awkwardly in her seat and tried to stretch her legs a little.

"You're pretty quiet tonight." He kept his eyes on the road as he spoke.

"Yeah, I guess it's because I had such a crazy week. I just need to wind down a little," Donna explained, and turned toward him. "I had to close out the third quarter, and though that's not a big deal for just the Hollywood store, since we've expanded, it's a real pain in the butt."

"I can imagine. I read that article in *Business* about Taylor-Made's expansion last week. Sounds like you two have done an incredible job." Jonathan glanced in his side mirror as he turned left onto West Pico Boulevard.

Donna didn't answer. She looked out the window and thought of everything that had happened this past week. No sense in dwelling on it, she thought. With a sigh she settled deeper into the seat.

"What's the heavy sigh for? Am I boring you?"

"Oh, no, I'm sorry, Jonathan. I was just thinking about some work problems. It has nothing to do with you." Donna touched his arm lightly. He smiled at her in the darkness.

"We're almost there. I hope you're hungry."

"Starved," she answered, surprised to find that she was actually telling the truth. Time had been so tight today, she hadn't stopped working to get anything to eat.

"Good, the food is excellent here." He pulled to the curb beside a small, windowed restaurant tucked in between two office buildings. The dark green awning above the door read LE PETIT ALGER.

Donna waited until Jonathan opened the door, then swung her legs out as she attempted to hoist herself from the seat. He reached over and grabbed her hand, pulling her free. "Great car, but a little difficult to get out of in a dress," she joked, and pulled her hemline lower.

"I never really thought about it, to tell you the truth." He grinned and held out his arm then moved smoothly to the door.

"What a gentleman," she murmured appreciatively as she slipped past him. Looks, money, intelligence, and manners! He definitely was too good to be true. The maître d' greeted him warmly and led them to a corner table set for two.

"Merci," Donna said as she sat down in the chair he held out for her. "This is really nice." She twisted around to look at the cozy room, filled with lace and greenery. The crystal stemware reflected hundreds of tiny candlelit flames. The room was filled with people, each table occupied, but somehow the atmosphere was subdued. Jonathan watched her, waiting for her reaction to his little hideaway. "I love it!" she exclaimed, and laid the deep evergreen napkin on her lap.

"I only bring special people here." He gazed at her pointedly, his eyes relaying a message.

Donna felt her palms grow sweaty and pulled her eyes away. "So how's business?"

The abrupt shift caught him by surprise, and for a split second Jonathan's face hardened. "Crazy," he answered smoothly. They sat in silence as several waiters appeared to pour water then drifted away. "Despite the recession my clients are always on the lookout for sound investments. We've been very fortunate this year."

"How long have you been a partner?" she asked as she sipped her water.

"Ten years! It's hard to believe it's been that long already."

She smiled. "I know what you mean. It's seems like only yesterday I was in still in business school, sweating my way through the M.B.A. program."

"How'd you end up at Wharton in the first place? I mean going east for school and everything?"

"It's funny really. When I was in high school at West Beverly, everyone thought I was your typical air-head. I mean, I had a lot of friends, but they all thought

I'd just marry some rich guy and continue living my life the way I did then."

"So what happened?" Jonathan asked as he placed his elbows on the table casually.

"One day, in business class, we started talking about the stock market and everyone had to build their own portfolio. It was all make-believe, but one of the guys talked me into doing it for real. So I did. We went in as partners and I found that I had an aptitude for numbers." Donna chuckled when she remembered how mad Steve had been after the smoke cleared. "We hit it big for about a week and I just had this feeling that it was time to sell. Well, my partner, Steve, had gotten bit by the bug and didn't agree. So I sold my shares and he lost everything."

Jonathan snickered. "Did he know?"

"I told him after he came to me saying it was my fault we didn't sell. You should have seen his face!"

"I can imagine," he said dryly.

"So after that I buckled down, and when graduation rolled around, I decided I wanted to make something of myself. Wharton had the best program." She shrugged as if it all made sense.

"You've really done an incredible job with Taylor-Made. I'm sure that Kelly is thrilled that you went to Wharton."

Donna frowned for a second. "I'm not sure what Kelly is these days," she said half under her breath.

"What do you mean?" He looked at her closely, curiosity evident in his eyes.

"Oh, it's nothing really. Just every once in a while Kelly does a disappearing act and it always seems to happen when I need her most."

"Really," he murmured, and took a drink. "I would have thought from what Solly told me that you two were the best of friends."

"We are. But that doesn't mean that I always agree

with the way she runs the business." Donna grew flustered under his unbending gaze. "Kelly is a good friend, probably one of the best I'll ever have. It's just that sometimes she takes advantage and leaves me holding the bag."

"So why don't you tell her?"

"If I knew where she was, I would." Her hand flew to her mouth in surprise. "I didn't mean to say that."

"It's okay, Donna, I'm not going to tell anyone," he promised. "I think we should place our orders now anyway, don't you?"

She smiled at him gratefully then listened as he effortlessly gave the captain their orders in fluent French. The meal passed quickly as Jonathan talked about his company and what his job entailed. Donna listened in fascination as he spoke about the financial rewards he had accrued, not only for his clients, but for himself.

"That's unbelievable!" she exclaimed as he finished.

"It sounds like it is, but it's not. It's actually very simple if you have the right people working for you."

"How do you find employees? I assume that you only settle for the best." She placed her napkin on the table and sat back in the padded chair.

"Referrals, or sometimes through acquaintances. I've found that to be one of my best recruiting areas." Jonathan grinned and flagged down a waiter.

Donna stared at him as he spoke, feeling herself drawn in. As if he could sense her watching, Jonathan reached across the table and stroked the top of her hand. She sat frozen, afraid to move and yet wanting to respond. His hand was large and muscular, its warmth reaching up her forearm. She moved her fingers tentatively, then tried to turn her palm upward so she could touch him. Her cheeks blazed as she realized he was watching and she pulled away.

"Thank you for dinner, it's been wonderful," she said hastily.

"It's not over yet," he replied as the waiter reappeared with a bottle of Cristal champagne and two glasses. "I have a proposition for you."

Donna's brown eyes sparkled. This was turning out better than she could have ever imagined. Brenda would die! She swallowed nervously and smiled at him.

"How would you like to come with me?" Jonathan questioned as he handed her a glass.

Donna looked at him in confusion. "Come with you where?" Did he really expect her to take off with him after one dinner?

"Over to Powell and Rosenfield." His voice was low and Donna had to lean forward to hear him. "I'll give you a senior vice-presidency with full stock options and you'll never have to worry about being left holding the bag again." He smiled self-importantly as he finished.

Donna's jaw fell open as she realized what he was offering. She sat up straight and stared into his eyes. "What are you talking about, Jonathan?"

"I'm offering you a job, Donna. Come work for me and I'll be sure that everything you could ever want is taken care of." He reached for her hand again.

"Don't." She moved her hands protectively into her lap. "I think that we have some crossed lines here." She smiled uneasily. "I'm very flattered by your offer, but I don't know why you would think I was up for grabs."

"Donna, you just sat here a little while ago telling me how Kelly disappears on you whenever things needed to be done. That's fine—if it was your name above the door. I don't have to point out to you that it's not." He ran his hand down the length of his tie and straightened his jacket.

Donna shook her head. "I'm sorry if you think I sent out a mixed message here, Jonathan, but I have no intention of leaving Taylor-Made. Don't think I'm not flattered; I am. I really appreciate your offer, it's extremely generous, and I'm sure that there's someone else who would kill for this opportunity. But my loyalty lies with Kelly, and even if things aren't always smooth between us, that's where I want to stay. At least for a while." Her voice had an edge to it, but she managed to smile sweetly across the table.

Jonathan toyed with his glass for a minute then looked up at her. "I think you are making a huge mistake here. Look at what I'm saying to you. Think about it, Donna. Stock options, all the perks . . . anything." He held his hands out suggestively.

She eyed him carefully, not letting him see the anger seething beneath the surface. "Anything . . ." She nodded as if she were seriously considering his comment. "Jonathan, here's the difference between you and me. You are obsessed with money, power, and status. I've never paid much attention to it. I guess it comes with growing up around superficial people. I've learned a lot of things in my life, and I guess the most important thing was who my friends are. To me, that means everything." She pushed her chair away from the table and stood looking down at him. "Friendship is more important than the bottom line, Jonathan; you should try it."

Donna slipped her purse onto her shoulder and started to walk away. Suddenly she stopped and turned back toward the table, raising her voice. "Pity about the champagne, Jonathan, it's such a waste!" She tossed her head and continued through the room as surprised diners craned their necks to see who she was speaking to. Jonathan sat silently at the cluttered table, his steepled fingertips covering the lower part of his face. He kept his eyes on the empty chair in front of him as if, by staring hard enough, he could will Donna to return. Not a chance, she thought as she put her coat on and set out to find a cab on the boulevard. Not a chance!

■   ■   ■

"Whoa! Watch out!" Dylan yelled appreciatively. He nodded his approval as Donna sat down laughing.

"What a slimebucket!" Brenda exclaimed. "I just knew there would be something shifty about that guy. He was way too perfect."

"Yeah, I said he was too good to be true from the beginning," Donna agreed.

"That was really great how you went to business school, Donna. Have you ever actually thought about it?" Andrea asked quietly.

"Sometimes I think of how cool it would be to do something like that, but with my grades I don't think I'd get in," she replied.

"Well, you definitely wouldn't get in on originality, that's for sure." Kelly kicked sand at her playfully and laughed. "You stole my fantasy! I can't believe you did that!"

Donna smiled meekly. "It was the only thing I could come up with on short notice; sorry. Besides, your idea was so hot, I just had to use it. Just think if we could really do something like that."

"Come on, you two. Let's have a little reality check here, okay?" Brandon interrupted. He groped through the remaining bag of potato chips. "Anybody have more chips stashed somewhere?"

"Brandon, would you stop worrying about your stomach for a while. That is so rude!" Brenda ripped the bag out of her brother's hands and rolled it up.

"Hey, what are you doing?"

"B., drop it, man. We're talking about Donna's fantasy here," Dylan reminded him.

"So what does that have to do with anything?" he asked as he looked around the circle. "All I want is a few more chips, what's the big deal?"

Andrea groaned beside him. "Would you just put a clamp on it, Brandon?"

Donna smiled at Andrea then turned to Brandon.

"We could actually do something like that, Brandon, you never know. What makes you think we couldn't?"

"I just can't see you two sacrificing your nightlife to build a business, that's all," he said defensively. "I didn't mean that it could never happen."

"But you think that you can take off to Europe and become the heartthrob to all women, right?" Kelly smirked and cocked her head at him.

"Well, now that you mention it, the odds are in my favor."

Kelly reached over and ripped her baseball cap off his head. "Dream on, Superstar."

Donna giggled. "You know, Brandon, you should never underestimate the power of a woman. That's how you always get yourself in trouble."

Brandon stared back at her, a wounded look on his face. "What's that supposed to mean, Donna?"

"Just that once a woman puts her mind to something, she usually gets it, that's all," she answered offhandedly, and smiled knowingly at Kelly and Brenda.

"And maybe between you and Kelly, you'll come up with one complete brain, right?" Steve snickered as he reached into the cooler.

"Very funny, Steve."

"I know." He settled back on the blanket and glanced around at his friends. "So who's next for the executioner's chair? Silver?"

David nodded anxiously and cleared his throat. "Yeah, it's my turn. Unless of course, Andrea would like to go first."

"No thanks, David. I'll just wait for my turn." Andrea smiled encouragingly at him as she reached for a stick to move a piece of wood deeper into the flames. "Go ahead."

He rubbed his hands across his thighs, his cheeks stained with nervous color. "So it's got to be ten years after graduation, right?"

"Come on, Silver, quit stalling. You know the rules," Dylan chided as he leaned back on his elbows casually.

"I was just checking, Dylan."

Everyone laughed as David unbuttoned his shirt collar. "Fire's pretty warm, isn't it?"

"David, would you just start?" Donna tugged at his sleeve impatiently.

"All right. Jeez, a guy can't even get a break around here."

The girls laughed as David closed his eyes for a second, trying to visualize what he would want his life to be like. If he could have anything, what would he want to do? Then it hit him.

"Okay, you guys all know how much I like working with video, right?"

Steve rolled his eyes at Brandon then leaned over. "He's probably going to be like a Rona Barrett or something," he said in a loud whisper. Brandon cracked up, then sat up straight when Andrea jabbed him in the side.

"You're supposed to be listening, remember?" she said reprovingly. Her glasses reflected the fire, making her seem possessed.

"Andrea, I don't know what your problem is tonight—"

"I don't have a problem," she interrupted. "Now just let David talk, will you?" She turned from him abruptly and folded her arms across her chest.

"Looks like you ticked her off in a major way, Minnesota." Dylan's face was expressionless as he gestured toward Andrea.

"Yeah, it seems like everything I do these days ticks her off," Brandon said wearily, shaking his head. He tossed a stick into the fire, only half listening as David vividly described his college days after West Beverly.

David

THE STAGE LIGHTS ADDED TO THE STIFLING
warmth of the auditorium, but David basked in the
heat as he stood waiting for the thunderous applause to
die down. His boyish face was flushed with excitement,
a wide grin from ear to ear. Finally his moment had
come, the one he had always dreamed about and
thought would never happen. The elegantly dressed
audience was on its feet, the noise level rising as he
bowed humbly to unseen faces in both directions.
There was only one thing missing from the moment—
the man who had believed in him from the start.

The wind whipped across the deserted parking lot
as David bent his head to his chest, a thermos of coffee
tucked under one arm. Intuitively he made his way in

the direction of the door. The first light of day poked through the heavy gray clouds as he shoved his key into the lock and pulled hard. The rusty hinges creaked in protest. "Come on," he said to himself, fighting against the wind. He managed to slip through the small opening just before the steel door slammed behind him.

Silence greeted him in the darkened hallway. "Where is everybody?" he wondered out loud as he checked out the shadowy editing rooms, turning on lights as he went. "I know we were supposed to start the loops at six-thirty."

David stopped suddenly as he looked up at the clock ticking on the wall. Five-forty-five. Great! He must have screwed up the alarm again. Might as well make the best of it, he thought as he took off his worn blazer and threw it over a nearby chair. Uncapping the thermos, he poured coffee into a paper cup he found in the dirty, cramped kitchen. The wind filtered through the numerous cracks in the walls and David pulled up his collar against the cold drafts.

Being a production assistant on a grade-B horror movie was definitely not the way to find fame and fortune in Hollywood; David had learned that quickly. They didn't tell you that in film school, though. After graduation David had thought it would be a piece of cake to find a job in the industry but to get anywhere, you had to know someone or have some credits. Too proud to ask his father for help, he had swallowed his pride and managed to land this job on a slasher flick. It wasn't a big-money production, but it paid the bills and gave him some background.

David sauntered back to the editing room, thinking about the day's work ahead. Looping was tedious work, but it was a specialized skill that took years to hone. Just one wrong splice and the entire film was choppy. It was an area that he needed work in and he was looking forward to watching Ben Garr do his magic. Forty years in the business and Ben's hands were flawless. David couldn't believe that he would actually work on a project as lowbrow as *Deadly Demons*.

Ben had laughed at David's surprise. "In this business, kid, you take whatever comes your way and you do your best with it. If you're too picky, you'll never make a living." David had listened carefully and then followed the balding man into the editing room. He had spent hours looking over Ben's stooped shoulder as Ben patiently explained different techniques and the reasoning behind his cuts. By the day's end David felt he had learned more from Ben than he had in all his years at film school. Eight weeks into production and he felt like Ben was an old friend. He couldn't wait to get started today, but another glance at the clock told him he'd have to fill a half hour before the others started to arrive.

He poured more coffee then wandered down the hallway, checking out the empty rooms. Sound stages and production offices dominated the large warehouse, each one varying only slightly from the one before. At the end of a short hallway an old wooden door stood partially open. Curious, David walked over and found himself in an old storage room, the shelves littered with bound scripts and old film canisters.

"Cool!" he exclaimed as he pulled out a rickety chair from underneath a console board and climbed up unsteadily.

A mouse skittered across the dusty shelf, squealing as it ran. David jumped back and almost fell off the chair. "Whoa!" he yelled as he regained his balance. "I think I better turn on the lights." He climbed down and found a switch, the single bulb adding only a dull yellow glow to the room. "Better than nothing," he mumbled, and started to shuffle through the scripts. None of the titles was familiar and David assumed that the movies must have been in development years ago and set aside. He grabbed a stack and started to flip through the yellowed pages.

Most of the projects were substandard and he chortled as he pictured some long-dead studio chief making mincemeat out of the unfortunate writers. "This is not what I pay you for," he spouted in a throaty voice, reaching up to put the scripts back on the shelf. Then he stopped. Tucked into the corner under two rusting film canisters sat a leather-bound sheaf of papers. David picked it up tentatively, his fingers caressing the aged surface of the cover. *"Final Fadeout,"* he read out loud as he jumped down from the chair and opened the script. Interesting title.

As the silence settled around him David lost track of time and didn't hear Ben yelling loudly in the hallway about unreliable staff. He didn't even notice when the mouse came slithering out of its hiding place, tricked by the quietness. The only things David saw were the stiff pages in front of him, and in his mind's eye, the beginning of a project he couldn't walk away from.

"Yeah, I know it's hard to get major distribution, but Ben, I'm telling you, this script has something," David pleaded to the leery film editor.

Ben rubbed his grizzled chin thoughtfully. "Okay, kid, let me take a look at it. I'm not promising you anything," he warned, "but let me see what I think of it."

David whooped and slapped Ben's shoulder enthusiastically. "Just wait till you read it, you'll see what I'm talking about. There's something there, I'm telling you!"

"Don't get too excited there, David. Just because I might agree with you doesn't mean this will ever see the light of day. I've seen a lot of great projects end up just where you found this one. Gathering dust in a closet."

"You won't feel that way after you've read it. But we need to find out where it came from. There's no writing credit anywhere." David flipped through the front pages quickly.

"Probably someone on salary to the studio in the heyday just banged it out. Lots of these old scripts are like that." Ben swung around in his chair, facing the editing board. "Listen, hotshot, we still have some work to do here. Do you think you can forget about *Final Fadeout* long enough to help me out?"

David was jerked out of his reverie. "Sure, Ben. Listen," he said as he sat down in the chair next to Ben's. "I didn't mean to be so late in helping with the loops. I just got sidetracked."

"I've heard four times already, Silver, will you drop it?" Ben punched some buttons on the console and waited for the tape to advance. "Let's put this baby to rest before you go trying to find another one, deal?"

David nodded. He listened as Ben gruffly called out instructions, his hands moving rapidly across the board. Four minutes of space left and over sixteen minutes of footage. It was going to be tight and concentration was essential. Reluctantly David put the script out of his mind and focused on the task in front of him. He grimaced as he watched the female lead decapitated in a shower of blood and sinew. There was definitely a better way to make a living, he thought to himself as he watched the frames fly by.

"The budget is too tight," David complained to Ben as they discussed financial details with their studio-assigned executive producer. It had been a hard road to get here, but with the backing finally in place they were just about to start preproduction on the movie.

"It's a generous budget for a first-time effort from an unknown, David." Peter Sorano spoke softly, but his words contained a message that David resented hearing.

He eyed the other man squarely, trying to detect a lack of support for the project. "Are you saying I'm a risk, Peter?"

"Frankly, yes, I am. I'm not going to pull any punches here, Silver. If this movie goes belly up, it'll be my head on the platter. You really don't have anything at risk." Peter frowned across the table, his tanned forehead full of crevices. His burgundy sweater seemed to lend authority to his presence, playing off the silver strands in his hair. "My entire reputation is on the line, do you understand?"

Ben nudged him under the table several times until David nodded curtly. He didn't mean to seem unreasonable, he just wanted *Final Fadeout* to get the treatment it deserved. He knew that he was lucky to have gotten this far with it, but he still resented being labeled an unknown. Since he had found the script in the production house two years earlier, David had done work on five films, two of which were currently major box-office hits. He had done his time, working alongside some of the best directors in the business, and now he wanted the chance to prove himself.

"Peter, let me just make one thing clear. I know that I should be thankful for getting this far, but if the studio didn't see any promise in the project, I wouldn't have, right? You've got your role to play and I have to see that this movie gets filmed in the best way possible. We have sixteen weeks of shooting ahead of us, let's start out on a positive note." David held his hand out amicably and grinned when Peter hesitated. "I'm serious, let's shake on it." Ben covered his mouth with his hand, his eyes betraying his mirth.

"Now I can see how you managed to pull this thing

together," Peter replied as he took David's hand. "You're smooth."

"I learned from the best," David said, laughing as he thought of Ben shouting ferociously at cowering production assistants and best boys. He turned to his partner and winked. "What do you say we plow through these figures and call it a day, Peter?"

Peter grinned, his ivory teeth a sharp contrast to his dark skin. "Sounds good to me. We've got a long road ahead of us and we should enjoy any free time we have before things get crazy."

"You can say that again," David replied, his eyes glittering. He couldn't wait to get started.

"Now, we need to keep everything under ten million, including salaries. I know you both had Jennifer Allyns in mind for the lead, but I don't think we can afford her. She'd eat into your budget and I don't think it's worth it."

David chuckled. "I already got her."

Ben's mouth fell open as David shrugged offhandedly.

Peter looked at him strangely. "How?"

"I went to the set of *Desperate Angels*, introduced myself, and told her that I was interested in working with her. She was really cool. She had me send over a copy of the revised script and then we had dinner." David watched as both of the men's faces filled with disbelief.

"You had dinner with Jennifer?" Peter shook his head. "How much is she asking for?"

"Half her normal fee. She loved the story line, and when I told how I wanted to direct it, she asked if we could make a deal. By the next morning I sent a contract over to her agency." David wiped his hands breezily. "Nice, nice."

"Do you realize what that will do for us?" Peter's voice grew shrill. "She has major drawing power. This

is fantastic! Silver, if this is just the beginning of what you two guys can pull off, I think that *Final Fadeout* is going to attract a lot of attention." He pounded his fist against the wooden table excitedly.

"That's what I've been trying to tell everyone all along, right, Ben?" David quipped. He beamed as Peter stared at him in admiration.

"I'll pick up the tux on my way home to shower," David explained as he looked out his office window. He nestled the phone on his shoulder as he flipped aimlessly through a copy of *Premiere* magazine.

"I'll be ready by five, all right? That way we'll get to the auditorium before the crush. How are you holding up? Okay?" Jennifer dropped her husky voice to a whisper.

David grinned into the phone. "I'm doing great. Are you kidding? My first time directing and the movie's nominated for seven Oscars—I feel like I'm in a dream."

Jennifer sighed anxiously. "I just hope you win. You really deserve it."

"Jenn, just the fact that I got nominated is enough for me. That and having you with me." He pictured her dressing as they talked, her long, golden-brown hair wet from the shower. She always looked so young then, her skin glowing and her brown eyes as soft as velvet. The little beauty mark on the side of her lip added a sense of mischief to her innocence. David felt himself grow warm and broke his train of thought. "So I'll see you in a little while, right?"

"I'll be waiting," she answered, and hung up.

He swung around and placed the phone down on his desk. The sun bounced off the tinted windows, adding little light to the stark whiteness of his office. Framed stills lined the walls, covering his brief work history in the

world of cinema. David smirked impishly at the expanse of the room and walked over to the windows. No matter how successful *Final Fadeout* was, he still couldn't believe it had happened. He wasn't too optimistic about his chances about winning best director; he was up against some heavies. But just the feeling of acceptance that went with the nomination was more than he had ever imagined. Here he was, only twenty-eight years old, and riding on the waves of success. The insistent buzz of the intercom brought him out of his musing.

"Yeah, Lisa?" he said brusquely into the receiver.

"Your car is outside. If you hurry, you should be able to make it before the rush starts."

"Thanks." He hung up then looked down at the papers he had been trying to tackle and shook his head. "These will just have to wait," he murmured to himself as he picked up his briefcase and walked out the door.

The crowds outside the Dorothy Chandler Pavilion stood patiently in the heat of the late-afternoon sun. Red velvet cords lined the wooden barriers holding them back. Cheers broke out each time another limousine pulled up, its occupants unaware of their effect. An announcer stood to one side, in front of all the press members, and identified the new arrivals as they appeared.

David had his window half-down as they waited in the long line of stretches. He tapped his fingers against his thigh nervously as he listened to each swell of applause. He pulled his collar as if it were biting.

"Getting a little nervous?" Jennifer asked quietly. She sat beside him, her long legs peeking out the slit of her cherry-red evening dress. His heart skipped as he looked at her. The soft curve of her lips was accentuated by crimson lipstick.

"You are gorgeous," he answered, leaning toward her and touching his lips against hers lightly. The heady smell of watermelon and spices made his mouth water.

"David, I think you better sit up," Jennifer mumbled into his ear. "We're next."

He sat up with a start and adjusted the front of his shirt. Little beads of perspiration popped out on his upper lip and he ran his finger across it hurriedly. As the car rolled forward he pushed the "close" button for the window. He wanted to act like he was in complete control. The sudden cheers of the crowd coincided with the limousine coming to a full stop. David grabbed Jennifer's hand tightly and waited for the door to open.

The next minute he was standing in the glare of the setting sun, adjusting his eyes to the brightness. Jennifer stood beside him, smiling demurely into the eyes of the cameras. They made a striking couple, her bare shoulder resting against the silkiness of his Versace tux. Murmurs of appreciation spread through the crowd as they started to walk toward the entrance.

The announcer kept time with their approach, reading off each of their credits and nominations as they drew near. The hoots and cheers grew in volume. David grinned widely and turned to wave at the crowd before they disappeared into the auditorium.

"What a rush!" he whispered to Jennifer as they followed their escort along the corridor. She smiled at his excitement and held her finger to her lips.

"Don't let anyone hear that you're enjoying this. That's a major faux pas. Everyone who's somebody acts like the Oscar ceremony is just an annual pain in the butt. A lot of prancing and preening with the Academy always ending up voting for the safe ones." She flipped her hair away from her face and looked over at him.

"Do you feel that way?" he asked uncertainly.

"Are you kidding! I still get a thrill riding in a limo." She ran her fingers through his hair affectionately. "I may be more experienced at this kind of thing, David, but I haven't forgotten where I came from."

He stopped at the door and held it open for her. As she breezed through he followed, his eyes focused on her red figure floating down the aisle. People turned to stare at Jennifer as she passed by, their expressions echoing his own every time he looked at her. He couldn't stop the smirk that spread across his face. He had definitely arrived.

"Here you are, sir," the usher said firmly, directing David into the crowded row.

"David, you both look fantastic." Peter Sorano stood and grabbed his hand eagerly, pecking Jennifer lightly on the cheek. "You holding up okay?"

"A little uptight, but I'm sure I'll be fine. How about you?" David looked over Peter's shoulder and waved at Peter's wife, sitting quietly watching the conversation.

"Not too bad. If anything, I think the fact that we're even here tonight as nominees is nothing short of a miracle. Are you going to Spago later?" Peter sat down as they moved toward their seats next to his.

"Probably. You?" David looked down on his executive producer. They'd had a tough beginning, but despite their differences they had managed to pull it off and had become close friends.

"We'll make an appearance. Marge can't stay out too late, with the new baby and all." Peter lowered his voice noticeably. "Feedings are tough to handle when you're exhausted."

David laughed and turned to Jennifer, who was coolly staring at people in the audience. "Who are you looking for?"

"No one in particular. I just wanted to get an idea of who's here. I used to think that you could predict

the winner by who wasn't in the audience." She snickered. "Silly, huh?"

"Nothing about you is silly," he answered, lifting her hand to his lips. Suddenly the lights grew dim and the ceremony began. As the music swelled, David felt his palms grow sweaty and pulled his hand away from Jennifer's. Get a grip on yourself, Silver! he thought, panicking. Taking deep breaths of air, he tried to quiet the erratic dance of his pulse. He closed his eyes and pretended that he was back in his office, but nothing seemed to work. As the minutes passed he only seemed to become more anxious.

"It'll be over before you know it," Peter whispered, and patted his arm sympathetically.

David tried to smile in the darkness, but his lips were locked in a straight line. This couldn't be happening. Here it was the biggest night of his life and he had developed lockjaw. Just relax, he told himself. The presentation of awards continued, and as he watched others around him get up to claim the coveted statue, David felt a sense of calm come over him. He probably wouldn't win anyway.

Jennifer remained unfazed, casually watching the proceedings. If he didn't know better, he would never have believed that she was up for Best Actress. As the presenters ran through the nominees, showing clips of the individual performances, David held Jennifer's hand, but couldn't look at her. "And the winner is . . . let me see here. Jennifer Allyns, *Final Fadeout*.

David jumped to his feet, bringing her with him as he crushed her to his chest to mumble into her hair, "Congratulations, Jenn, I love you."

She kissed him quickly then strode up on stage to collect her award. People applauded wildly as she zoomed past, her brown hair flying behind her. His eyes blurred as he felt his chest swell with pride as she spoke into the microphone. "Most importantly, David, this is

for you!" she finished as she held the golden figure aloft.
He clapped loudly as she exited the stage, stopping only
when he realized he was the only person left standing.

"Now if we can keep the good luck rolling," Peter
said dryly as they adjusted themselves in their seats.
David nodded and looked to see if Jennifer was making
her way back yet. Both aisles from the stage were
empty and he sat back in his chair, knowing she'd
probably be stuck backstage for a bit. After a few more
awards, she returned, apologetic but ecstatic. "I can't
believe I won!" she whispered as she scooted past him.

"Are you kidding? You deserved it! No one could
hold a candle to your performance. Jenn, I'm so proud
of you," he exclaimed, and hugged her.

"But I owe it all to you, David," she whispered as
she held on to his arm. "If you hadn't approached me
like you did, I wouldn't be here."

He held her eyes, trying to engrave the moment in
his memory until Peter grabbed his jacket. "Looks like
you're up," Peter said in a low voice.

David fell back against his seat, the panic rising
again in his throat. The screen above the stage came
alive with clips from *Final Fadeout*. Gasps of surprise
and admiration surrounded him as they watched the cli-
mactic fiery explosion, where Jennifer's character
jumps from a burning movie set. It was good, he
couldn't deny it. Her face was framed by the red-orange
inferno, acceptance of her death evident in her empty
eyes. He clenched his teeth as the clip came to an end,
Jennifer's hand resting on his thigh. He tried to concentrate as other film clips appeared, but all the words
seemed to run together. He attempted a smile as the
presenters walked to the podium, the ivory envelope in
hand. TV cameras panned the nominees, capturing
their expressions for the millions of home viewers.

"The winner of the Best Director award is . . .
David Silver, *Final Fadeout*!"

The soundtrack blasted through hidden speakers on cue as David kissed Jennifer soundly on the lips, drawing her close to him. Her eyes were filled with tears as she let his hands slip away to hug Peter.

"You did it, man! You actually did it!" Peter swung him from side to side, reluctant to let David go.

Cheers erupted from the audience as he dashed up the aisle, his jacket flapping in the air. David touched eager hands that reached out to him, not seeing who was greeting him. As he ran up the stairs two at a time, the audience came to its feet, applauding as he rushed toward the podium. He stopped and bowed twice, then continued. The statue glowed in the harsh lights, beckoning him. As he reached for it the first thought that ran through his head was how small it really was. He clutched the award in his hand as he waited for the applause to fade. By squinting, he could see past the first rows and locked his eyes on Jennifer. She blew him a kiss of encouragement, then sat back to listen.

"Thank you . . . thank you very much." He could hear his voice echoing off the far walls, making him feel like the wizard of Oz. He took a deep breath to calm himself, then smiled. "You spend all of your life thinking of this day and what you'll say, but when it actually happens, everything you had wanted to say is gone." He paused for the soft laughter that reached up to him. "I can't believe this is happening. . . ." Cheers greeted his statement and David shook his head then swallowed, trying to focus on what he had to say.

"When I first discovered the script for *Final Fadeout*, I brought it to the film editor I was working under at the time. He was an old, crotchety guy, always yelling and screaming." David chuckled as he pictured Ben in his mind. "But he was also one of the best editors in the business and he taught me a lot. He told me to fight for this movie if I believed in it, so I did—with a little politic help from Ben. I wish that Ben Garr was

still around to see this." He patted the gold body tenderly, tears brimming in his eyes. Ben had passed away three months after they had finished production. David coughed then continued.

"There are so many people to thank, so bear with me. Uh, I'd like to thank my parents, who put up with me all those years I drove them crazy with the video camera. My executive producer, Peter Sorano, who never told me no again after our first meeting." David smiled in Peter's direction. "Jennifer Allyns, who made *Fadeout* as good as it is. You're beautiful, Jenn!" A spotlight fell on her tearstained face, capturing the audience's attention as applause broke out. "Thanks to all the hard workers we had on location, it really was worth the sweat! And last of all I'd like to thank some really good friends of mine from West Beverly. Donna, Brandon, Kelly, Brenda, Dylan, and Steve—wherever you are, thanks for everything. Even when it looked like things couldn't get worse, you guys always said I could make it. Thanks a lot!" David raised the statue in a salute and sidestepped toward the stairs, smiling at the thunderous applause rolling toward him. Someone touched his elbow, guiding him toward the shadows backstage. With one last wave David followed, the cheers reverberating in his head. Just like I always dreamed it would be, he thought as he found himself surrounded by well-wishers.

David stopped talking and looked around him, wondering why his friends weren't saying anything. "What?"

"Knowing you, Silver, you probably will do something like that," Brandon said, patting him on the shoulder.

"I can see it, no problem. You've got that attitude, man. You know, Mr. Hollywood," Dylan added, his face serious as he looked over at David.

"I think it's the sweetest thing I've heard all night," Donna stated as she leaned across and kissed David on the cheek. "Even if there is another woman in it." She batted her eyelashes at him seductively then giggled.

"What was the movie about, David? You never really told us." Kelly pursed her lips as she watched him.

"Uh, I don't know, a movie star who's being stalked by a crazed fan," he made up as he spoke.

"That's creepy!" Brenda squealed, and drew her legs up to her chest protectively.

"Sounds excellent to me," Donna said with a laugh. "I love scary movies!"

"We know," Kelly groaned, making a disgusted face at her friend.

"So, David, tell me. Where did this Jennifer come from? Is she completely from your imagination or is there actually someone like her walking around?" Brandon stretched his arms overhead then cracked his knuckles loudly.

"Uh, I made her up," David answered, his eyes darting around the circle. "Well, not exactly. She kind of looks like that girl in the soda commercial. . . ."

Dylan and Steve burst out laughing as Brandon nodded in understanding. "I know *exactly* who you're talking about."

"Who?" Donna asked Brandon, a blank look on her face.

"Never mind," Dylan interrupted, shaking his head. "It's just the male hormone taking over again."

Brenda grabbed Dylan's chin and pulled his face toward her. "Like you never do that, right?"

"Who me?" Dylan asked innocently.

"Forget about it, Brenda," Kelly warned. "He'll never tell you anyway. So, who's turn is it now? Yours, Andrea?"

Andrea nodded and pushed her glasses up on her nose. "Unless you guys want to call it a night? It is get-

ting kind of late," Andrea suggested as she glanced around at her friends.

"No way, Andrea, you aren't getting off that easy. We still have a few pieces of wood here to burn." Brandon picked up a couple of the small branches and tossed them into the low flames. "What are you, in a hurry or something?"

Andrea stared at him, her face set in a stony expression. "No, Brandon, I have all the time in the world." She reached for her gold sweatshirt and pulled it down over her head then yanked her curly hair out from under the collar. "Much better! Now where was I?"

"You were trying to weasel out of telling us your fantasy," Steve reminded her. He snickered as Andrea glared at him.

"Fine. So after graduation I went to Yale," Andrea began.

"Of course, it has to be an Ivy League school," Brandon interrupted.

"Brandon!" Kelly and Brenda yelled at the same time.

Dylan chuckled as Brandon ducked his head under his arms protectively. Minnesota was definitely not doing too well in the popularity contest tonight, he thought as he watched Andrea across the fire. He casually wrapped his arms around Brenda as he pictured what it would be like to care about someone, but not be able to tell them. He couldn't believe that Brandon didn't see what was really going on. Maybe he'd figure it out soon . . . but then again sometimes Brandon could be so dense! Dylan shook his head and smirked.

Andrea

ANDREA ZUCKERMAN SHOVED A LARGE BUNCH of papers into her worn leather briefcase and looked up at her boss woefully. "I understand your concerns, Ron, but I really can't talk about it right now." She shook her wrist out of her sleeve and frowned at her watch. "I'm already twenty minutes late for an appointment."

Ron's face darkened. "Another publishing meeting by any chance, Andrea?"

She didn't answer as she hurriedly cleaned off her desk. She had worked with Ron Rivello for the past four years and they had always had a great relationship—until five weeks ago.

"Aren't you going to answer me?" he prodded.

Andrea slammed a stack of reference books on a side table and swung around. "Why do you have to

make this so difficult? I would have thought you'd be thrilled for me, supportive of any opportunities that came my way. Ever since I got the Pulitzer, you've been treating me like I'm the lowest class of life-form on this planet."

He studied her for a second then said, "Ever since you got the Pulitzer, you've been acting like all those pretentious people we used to make fun of." Ron folded his arms and leaned against the edge of her desk.

"I can't believe you would say that! What is the matter with you?" Andrea shook her head and reached over to pull her coat off the back of her chair. It hurt her to see her friendship with Ron affected by the excitement of the award. He was one of her closest friends in New York and she didn't want to lose his friendship over this. "Ron, let's not fight, okay? I really need you to be there for me during all of this. I promise, after things calm down, we'll get together for dinner and talk it out, all right?"

"By the time things calm down for you, Andrea, I might not be here," he said as walked past her out the door.

"This is just great!" she mumbled as she turned off her office lights and hurried down the hall to the elevators.

Outside the gray concrete building Andrea bolted into the street, waving her arms to stop a passing cab. Jumping in, she leaned forward and said, "Sixty-seventh and Third, please." As the cab driver pulled into the heavy late-rush-hour traffic, she sat back and exhaled loudly, blowing her curly bangs up off her forehead. Life was definitely getting more complicated than it was worth, she thought as the cab turned up Park Avenue.

This would be her fourth meeting with interested publishers since her series of articles, *Running Scared,* had won a Pulitzer Prize. When she first started the

piece, she had never expected the acclaim it received
and she didn't know how to handle the sudden fame
that went along with it.

Andrea rubbed her forehead as she thought about
Ron and how hard it was on him. He had been her men-
tor ever since she had moved to the city, showing her
the ropes at the paper, introducing her to all the right
people. Now she seemed to have grown out of his world
and moved into another one. Andrea's eyes filled with
tears as she recalled his angry words. Maybe he was
right and she had changed. With a sigh she tried to put
everything out of her head for at least a few minutes.

"This corner here, miss?" the cabdriver asked
loudly as he looked at Andrea in his rearview mirror.

"Oh, yeah, thanks. Here you go." She handed him
the fare around the Plexiglas window and scooted out.
The sign for La Cerise was really just an engraved
bronze plaque and only the people who knew where to
look could find it. Andrea squinted and moved toward
the unassuming door, her palms growing sweaty. As
she walked into the foyer the rich aroma of exotic
spices tickled her nostrils. She stood uncertain by the
door, feeling more awkward than she had all those
years at West Beverly.

"Yes, madame, may I help you?" The dark-suited
maître d' appeared from behind a heavy red velvet curtain and looked at her with unconcealed curiosity. His
dark hair was slicked back from his forehead and
shimmered in the soft light.

"I'm supposed to be meeting someone, he's probably here already," she stammered under the man's
steady gaze.

"Your party's name?"

"Ashland. Jeff Ashland," she answered quickly.

A huge smile appeared on his wrinkled face.
"Monsieur Ashland, of course. You must be
Mademoiselle Zucker . . ."

"Zuckerman," she finished.

"Yes, Monsieur Ashland is at his table. Please, let me take your coat and bag for you." He helped her out of her coat then snapped his pudgy fingers twice in the air. A tuxedoed young man appeared instantly to take her belongings then slipped back behind the curtain. "Now if Mademoiselle will follow me, I'll take you to your table." He gestured toward an archway and walked quickly across the ivory marble floor, his light steps tapping against the hard tiles. Andrea kept her eyes locked on the small of his back, afraid that if she glanced around at her surroundings, someone would stand up and shout that she didn't belong here.

"Here we are, Mademoiselle, enjoy," he said as he guided her toward a small corner table surround by a red leather settee.

She smiled at him gratefully as Jeff Ashland stood up and held out his hand. "Andrea, I am so glad you could make it. I would like you to meet Jennifer Reese, one of our most talented editors at Crossman."

Andrea smiled shyly as she shook the young woman's hand. "I can't tell you how much I admire your writing," Jennifer said warmly. Her cheeks were dotted with tiny freckles, adding a touch of color to her milky skin, and her chestnut hair hung in a long, thick pageboy.

"Thank you, Jennifer, that's always nice to hear. You know us writers, we're basically the most insecure people in the world." As they all laughed Andrea slipped her legs under the table and moved across the red leather settee carefully. "I'm sorry I'm so late. I got tied up at the office and then traffic was pretty heavy."

"No need to apologize. It gave us an opportunity to discuss several projects we have coming up," Jeff said in his clipped British accent then cocked his head toward Jennifer. "Jen has just finished working on another nonfiction title that we have some high expectations for in the spring."

Andrea raised her eyebrows and said, "Anyone I know?"

Jennifer chuckled. "I don't think so. He's a Native American writer who lives on a reservation in New Mexico. It's about the Indian movement and their struggles."

"It sounds interesting," Andrea said, and studied the other woman. "Do you specialize in nonfiction?"

"No, I prefer some flexibility. Being an editor is such a subjective job that I think if I focused all my energy on one category, I would lose interest completely."

"And we definitely wouldn't want that to happen," Jeff said in an exaggerated tone. Jennifer made a face at him across the table. "Would like something to drink before we order, Andrea?"

"A seltzer with lemon would be great, thanks." Andrea looked down at the calligraphied menu before her, trying to focus on the entrées, while Jeff instructed the waiter. Between being exhausted and her increasing nervousness, she couldn't seem to stop her mind from wandering. "Any suggestions?" she asked brightly after a minute.

"I'm having the chicken. I had it the last time I was here and it was fabulous!" Jennifer pointed to the entrée on the menu. "It's made with mushrooms, garlic, some white wine, and spices. Just talking about it makes my mouth water."

"You sold me."

"Smashing; here, let me see." Jeff picked up his menu as a waiter looked over his shoulder. "Yes, I'll have the veal and red potatoes and the ladies are having the chicken in white wine."

"Yes, monsieur," the waiter answered, then gathered up the menus and hurried toward the kitchen.

"Now, where should we begin?" Jeff asked as he clapped his hands together. Andrea grinned at his earnestness.

"What would you like to know?" she said.

"What other kinds of writing have you done?" Jennifer inquired as she munched on a piece of bread.

"Mostly everything I've written has been for a newspaper. I haven't really had the time to try fiction. I did publish a couple of short stories back in school, but it seems that every time I try to write for myself, something comes up at work. I spend a lot of time researching my material beforehand," Andrea explained. "Then after I feel that I can converse knowledgeably about the subject, I sit down to write. It keeps me in touch with my topic."

"I'll say it does. I read the first article that appeared in the series on the train to work, and by the time I got to the office, I was filled with outrage at our justice system. I stormed in and slammed my office door so hard, my assistant wouldn't come near me for hours." Jennifer giggled.

"It really hits you, doesn't it?" Andrea responded.

"Because it can happen to any of us. Even you, Jeff. Men are also victims of stalkings. So don't play this he-man stuff with us, this is serious." She pointed at him as she spoke.

"I know it is! I read Andrea's material, too, you know," he answered defensively. Everyone fell silent as three waiters approached with their dinners, covered in polished silver domes. Without a word they served the table then slipped away.

"How did you come up with the focus of the articles, Andrea? It's not your usual front-page topic unless someone has been hurt. Then it becomes a tabloid story," Jennifer pointed out as she cut through a piece of the boneless chicken smothered in mushrooms.

"Actually my best friend was being stalked for years by this guy we went to high school with," Andrea explained patiently to the other woman. She had been telling this story repeatedly for weeks now and it was starting to wear on her.

"She didn't even know it at first." Andrea nodded as Jeff raised his eyebrow questioningly. "We were living together for a while and someone was calling at night and breathing heavily, then hanging up. It seemed harmless until her car was beaten in with a metal pipe one night while we were sleeping. After fighting with the phone company for a while, we got a tap on the phone. Then, after someone tried to break into our house, the police would drive by every other hour to make sure we were okay. We never found out who it was, and after I moved away, my friend got married.

"It wasn't until she was pregnant with her second child that it started again with the phone calls. Then he started talking, telling her how he knew that her son was really his and that she was really in love with him, not her husband." Andrea paused, watching as Jeff's face twisted with disbelief.

Jennifer froze, her fork midway to her mouth. "That's really sick!" she said in a firm voice. "People like that deserve to be put away."

"If only it worked that way, Jennifer. She got so scared of being alone with her kids, they finally had to get an order of protection against him. She and her husband went the court route—appearances, reports—the whole bit. After all that the judge finally ordered a psychiatric evaluation. The strangest thing about that is my friend was never told what the results showed. And this is a guy who was delusional for over ten years!"

"I can't believe that no one would tell her," Jeff said curtly, his accent deepening with his mounting frustration. "Has anything further happened?" He twisted the white linen napkin then tossed it to the side of his plate.

"Not yet. The order of protection only ran out a few weeks ago and she can't do anything else until he does. I guess she's at what you would call a stalemate with the guy. It's really amazing how archaic the judi-

cial system is in this country." Andrea leaned her elbows on the table, folding her hands, then rested her chin on top.

"How is she handling all of this?" Jennifer asked. "It must be awful to have to constantly look over your shoulder like that."

"It's become second nature to her. I'm not saying it's a healthy way to live, but it may be the only way she can protect herself at this point, always keeping her eyes open." Andrea pushed her dinner plate away distractedly.

"Until I starting reading your articles, I didn't realize how vulnerable women really are. Your friend, would she ever do anything violent?" Jeff's brown eyes were filled with concern.

"If it came down to protecting her children, yes, I think she would. This man isn't only a threat to her, he's a threat to her entire family." Her voice rose as she spoke, causing people to glance toward their table. Color stained her cheeks as she placed her hand over her mouth. "Sorry, I didn't mean to lose it on you; it's just I find this topic a bit close to home."

"It's quite all right, I can understand why you would react that way. It if was one of my closest friends, I would, too." Jeff smiled understandingly at her then toyed with his fork.

"I don't know what I would do if it was one of my friends!" Jennifer frowned as she spoke, her eyebrows furrowed above her dark eyes.

"Knowing you, Reese, you'd hunt him down!" Jeff teased his editor lightly.

Watching their easy camaraderie, Andrea noticed the silvery strands weaving through Jeff's brown hair. There was a look of kindness on his face, but she wondered if his sudden concern was just a ploy to convince her to sign a contract with his publishing company. In a short time Andrea had been exposed to every technique there was to woo a writer—from fancy, intimate

dinners to formal meetings with top executives. Despite her jadedness, Andrea sincerely felt that Jeff was somehow different. "Do you mind if I ask you a question, Jeff?" she interrupted.

"Not at all. Please, go ahead." He shuffled his feet under the table as he squared his shoulders.

Andrea fought the grin that teased her lips. His formal manner gave him a youthfulness that she found disarming. "Which case history really hit you the hardest out of the series?" She sat back and caught Jennifer's eye while Jeff thought hard about her question. "That one always catches them off guard," she whispered to the young woman. Jennifer grinned back then studied her boss.

When all the calls had started to come in from interested publishers, Andrea had vowed only to work with someone who truly cared about the plight of women whose orders of protection were just useless pieces of paper. In every meeting she tried to find out what type of reactions people had toward the articles and which they felt was the most disturbing case history. It gave her an opportunity to see whether the publisher truly considered the project itself more important than the fact she had won a Pulitzer Prize for the series.

"The young woman from Long Island, I believe," Jeff answered after a few moments. Andrea raised her eyebrows in interest. "I found it particularly disturbing that she had reached out for help repeatedly, and no one listened."

"Jeff, I am really impressed," Jennifer exclaimed. "Her case is a perfect example of why our judicial system needs a major overhaul."

Andrea nodded. "She had gone to the police the day before the incident."

Jeff struck his palm down on the table. "That's exactly what I'm talking about. Andrea, this book

needs to be written. I don't know what effect it could have on the actual legal aspect of these cases, but these women should be aware that they are not alone."

"I had planned to include a chapter of guidelines and a list of support groups, that type of thing," Andrea replied. "When I was doing my research, I contacted a lot of the hotlines and support groups, so I have plenty of information."

"Sounds good. How about doing a ten-step how-to guide for filing an order of protection, when it applies, and what type of protection it offers?" Jennifer added.

"Great idea!" Andrea exclaimed, then picked up her glass of water and took a gulp. She didn't want to seem too agreeable just yet.

"I did want to mention some of the successes we've had with nonfiction projects of this sort and what we could hope for with your project," Jeff said, then hesitated. "That's if you decide to publish with us, of course."

"Of course," Andrea mimicked.

"Right." His face was uncertain, but he continued. "In the past we've managed to propel a previously unpublished author to the number-one position on the best-seller list in several ways. The quality of your writing speaks for itself, but the key here is to get you out on the talk-show circuit." His face was animated, the mounting excitement evident in his eyes. "Your topic is both timely and compelling. It would make a perfect focus for talk shows. That could translate into sales of six figures or more."

"I don't want *Running Scared* to be sensationalized," Andrea said firmly. "That's exactly why all these cases have been ignored."

"We would be sure that it is treated with the respect it deserves," he reassured her. "Andrea, you already have credibility—not only because of the Pulitzer, but because of your professional background.

A Yale graduate, award-winning staff reporter for *The New York Times,* those are all impressive credits for such a young person." Jeff fidgeted nervously as he tried to backtrack, sensing her sudden defensiveness.

"What Jeff means is that the talk-show circuit wouldn't trivialize your message. It would effectively deliver it to millions of Americans across the country," Jennifer interjected.

"Exactly. We need to reach Middle America with this project, get them to wake up to what is happening around them," Jeff said.

Andrea listened with half an ear as he explained the marketing and promotional ideas that his executive team had put together quickly after she had agreed to meet with them. Though both Jeff and Jennifer had impressed her with their insight, it seemed that everyone wanted to make her into a media star and she wasn't sure that was what she wanted.

"We could also possibly stage a fund-raiser for one of these groups, a book-signing party or something. What do you think?" Jeff searched her face for some sign of enthusiasm.

Andrea twirled the crystal water glass in her hand, watching the shards of light dance along the cream-colored walls. Some of the most powerful players in New York were sprinkled throughout the softly lit room. Polished silver and exotic flowers decorated every table. She had never been at La Cerise before and was amused at how overrated it was.

"It sounds interesting . . . listen, Jeff, Jennifer, I'm going to be honest with both of you."

"We want you to be," Jeff interjected.

"Definitely," Jennifer added.

"Good." She smiled. "Okay, here goes. There's a lot of things happening right now that I never expected. No, hear me out," she said, holding her hand up as Jeff opened his mouth to speak. "Ever since I was a lit-

tle girl, I wanted to be a reporter. I lived and breathed to write. Soon it became everything to me. I even weasled my way into a school outside my district so that I could get a better education and get accepted at an Ivy League school. I'm not kidding," she said adamantly as they both grinned at her. "For four years I pretended I lived in Beverly Hills just so I could go to West Beverly High."

"It obviously paid off, though," Jeff commented, his brown eyes twinkling.

"What paid off was a lot of hard work. When I got the job at the *Times* I thought I had finally achieved what I had set out to get." She stopped and took a deep breath. "But I was wrong. Since I did that series, all these doors are opening and I don't know which one to choose. I feel like a contestant on 'Let's Make a Deal.'"

"Let's make a what?" Jeff asked, his brow furrowed until Jennifer nudged him in the side and made an exasperated face. "What did I do?"

Andrea chuckled at his lack of familiarity with American television. "It's just an old game show. Never mind. The point is, I think I need to take some time to think about everything for a while before I make any decisions." Her shoulders sagged as if they had been drawn taut by invisible strings that had suddenly snapped.

Jeff glanced at Jennifer, an unspoken message passing between them. He stared at Andrea for a minute then said, "Andrea, I think you should consider everything that's being offered to you and decide what's best for *you*. It has to be extremely overwhelming at this point. I just hope that when you're ready to make a decision, you keep us in mind. We would really love to work with you on this project. I mean that." He motioned to a passing waiter. "Would you ladies care for some coffee or dessert?"

"I couldn't eat another thing," Jennifer said as she

patted her flat stomach under her burgundy linen dress.

"Just coffee for me, please," Andrea replied, then sat quietly as Jeff discussed the dessert possibilities with the waiter. He had everything she was looking for in a publisher . . . or maybe she was just reacting to his charm, letting her loneliness control her brain again. He was cute, in a kind of cuddly way.

Now she knew it had been too long since her last date! Here she was sitting across from a man who was almost twenty years older, married, and from an entirely different world than hers, and all she could think about was how cute he was. If only her grandmother had lived to see this, she thought ruefully.

She smiled absently as Jeff excused himself from the table. As he meandered across the room he stopped to talk at several tables. One thing was for sure, Andrea thought as she watched him chatting, he knew how to work a room.

"I was talking with an author yesterday," Jennifer said as Andrea's mind wandered. She tuned out the young woman's voice and glanced around to see if she recognized any of the high and mighty that could afford to dine at La Cerise. Their corner table allowed her a view of the entire room.

Holding her coffee cup to her mouth, she scanned slowly with half-closed eyes, noting that the dominant age group was over sixty. The crisp white table linens played off the snowy crowns of a few of the men, as if they had been dipped in the same vat of bleach. Andrea chuckled.

"Something funny?"

"Oh, no, um, well . . ." Andrea stuttered. She had been so lost in her thoughts she hadn't noticed Jeff's return. "I was just looking at all of these people, wondering how they can afford to eat here. It's a bad habit I inherited from my grandmother. You stare at some-

one you don't know and try to picture what their lives
are like. Weird, huh?"

"A bit strange, I would have to say," he said with a
grin.

"It is not, Jeff, I do that, too! Especially on the sub-
way when you're squished in like sardines and you
can't help but stare at the person next to you," Jennifer
said as she wiped her mouth daintily with her napkin.

Jeff's face grew serious. "Andrea, I hope I didn't
make you feel pressured earlier."

"No, I think I'm just overloaded with these meetings and I'm sorry if I came down heavy on you. You've
been great." Andrea pushed her cup to the edge of the
table as a waiter breezed over to refill her coffee.

"Even if you sign with someone else for *Running
Scared,* I hope that we could do another project together. I truly do admire your writing." As if all bets were off
now that she had laid her cards on table, he loosened
his tie and sat back. She felt herself warming to his
smile as her eyes drifted to a point just beyond his head.

"Oh, my God!" she whispered, her eyes large
behind her wire-rim glasses.

"What? What's the matter?" Jeff asked, craning his
tousled head around.

Jennifer followed her line of vision and murmured
under her breath, "My, my, my!"

It was him! Brandon Walsh was sitting at a table
directly across the room with a sleek blond-haired
woman. Andrea's mouth grew dry and she grabbed her
water glass hastily. Five years had passed since she had
seen him, and he still looked the same. She ran her fingers nervously through her hair then wiped water
droplets from her lips, not taking her eyes off him. His
brown hair was long again, as it had been when he first
moved to Beverly Hills, the soft waves reaching down
the back of his neck. His fair skin was dark, as if he had
recently spent many hours baking in the sun.

"Andrea, are you okay?" Jeff's voice interrupted her assessment.

"Oh, yeah, sure. What were we talking about?" She sat up straight and pulled at the bottom of her shirt, wishing she had stuck to her diet.

"I just wanted you to know how much I want to work with you someday—"

Andrea's eyes locked onto Brandon's and an electric charge zoomed through her body down to her toes. A look of surprise crossed his face as he broke into a wide, pearly grin that stood out against his tan skin. He stood up and murmured something to his companion then started to hurry across the crowded room. The sounds of clinking silverware and muffled conversation faded as Andrea sat frozen, watching him approach.

"Andrea, is something wrong?" Jeff asked again as he watched her face drain of color. He turned in his chair just as Brandon walked up.

"Andrea, I can't believe it!" Brandon bent down and kissed her warmly on the lips. "You look fantastic! Congratulations, I just heard about the Pulitzer!"

"Brandon, how are you? What a surprise!" she said in a high-pitched voice. She had always pictured this moment in her mind and now she was speechless.

Jennifer leaned over and touched Andrea's arm. "Aren't you going to introduce us?" she said with a grin.

"Oh, of course, sorry. Brandon, this is Jeff Ashland and Jennifer Reese of Crossman Publishers," she replied.

"Pleased to meet you. Brandon Walsh. Andrea and I went to school together," he explained as he shook their hands.

"At Yale?" Jennifer asked as she looked up at him through her dark lashes. Andrea fought a sudden urge to kick her under the table.

"Nah, are you kidding? They wouldn't even look at someone like me," he answered with a smirk. His sky-

blue eyes sparkled with amusement. "We went to high school together at West Beverly."

"The school you told us about earlier," Jeff commented, looking over at Andrea.

"Yes." Her tone was abrupt, but she didn't want Brandon knowing she was still defensive about her background after all these years.

"I can just imagine what she told you," Brandon said with a mocking look. "Listen, I hope I'm not interrupting anything."

"Not at all." Jennifer moved over on the settee. "Why don't you join us?"

Andrea's stomach flipped as she watched Brandon's eyes take in Jennifer's curvy figure. "Thanks anyway," he said with a shake of his head. "I was just hoping I could have a word with Andrea alone." He looked at her questioningly.

Andrea glanced hesitantly at Jeff and Jennifer across the table. "If you both don't mind . . ."

"Of course not." Jeff waved off her question.

Andrea smiled gratefully at him as she slipped out of the booth and stood up. "I'll just be a minute."

"We'll be waiting," Jennifer said dryly, looking hard at Brandon, the invitation obvious in her eyes. He grinned then guided Andrea across the room.

"Where's your coat?" he whispered into her ear as he slipped his arm through hers.

"My coat? Why?"

"Why do you always have to ask questions?" He touched his lips to her forehead as they passed through the entranceway to the dining room.

Andrea went rigid, his kiss burning into her skin. Could this really be happening? she thought frantically as her feet moved woodenly beneath her. "Brandon, I don't know what you have in mind, but I left my purse back at the table."

"Great!" he said curtly as he stopped dead and

pulled away from her. "In case you haven't figured it out yet, Einstein, I'm trying to kidnap you." Andrea looked at him in confusion and Brandon snorted. "You know, sweep you up and take you away—that kind of thing. Andrea, I have wanted to do this since the first day we met. But you were always so uptight, I never tried. Seeing you here tonight after so long made me realize that it was now or never. If I didn't act now, you'd slip away again and I might not ever get the chance to tell you how I really feel."

"Oh," she uttered in surprise.

"And of course you manage to throw a wrench into my plans. Now that I think of it, you always used to do that." He frowned and rubbed his chin. "But hey, I'm not one to hold a grudge, so what do you say you go back and get your pocketbook, tell those honchos in there *hasta la vista,* and I'll meet you at the door. Is your coat in the coatroom?"

Andrea stood gaping, unable to believe her own ears. "Are you serious?"

"No, Andrea, I just dumped my date, who happens to be both rich and single," he said as he dodged her playful swing, "and took you away from your power meeting so we could hash over old times and compare war stories." Brandon laughed as he placed his hands on his hips and waited. "Well? What's it going to be?"

"Brandon, I can't just walk out! This is a business meeting," Andrea said, her eyes pleading.

"That's your problem, Andrea, you always are afraid to take a chance. You can do whatever you want to do, no one is going to stop you," Brandon answered. "Are you going to spend your life living the way other people expect you to or are you going to take a chance with me?"

Andrea hesitated then ran her hand across his cheek. There was no way she was going to let him get away this time. "You're right, Brandon, I'll be back in one second, promise!" She started to run backward

into the dining room and collided with a tall waiter, his arms lined with silver-globed dinners. The plates fell crashing to the tile floor, the noise echoing through the room. She wanted to disappear as she felt everyone turn to stare. "Ohmigod! I'm really sorry—I didn't hurt you? Here, let me help," she said as she bent down to pick up the shattered remains.

"Psst . . . Andrea, hurry up!" Brandon urged her from around the corner, trying to contain his laughter.

She met the waiter's eye and attempted a smile. "I'm really sorry about this, but I have to go."

"Please, mademoiselle, you have done enough already," he said with exasperation.

Andrea jumped up then pulled her skirt down awkwardly. Holding her head high, she marched toward the table where Jeff and Jennifer sat watching. "Uh, I have to leave, um, something came up," she stammered as she reached for her purse. She kept her eyes averted as she caught the knowing smirk on Jennifer's face. "Thanks so much for the dinner, it was great meeting you both."

"Is everything okay, Andrea? You seem rather flustered," Jeff asked as he rose from the table.

"Everything is fine," she said firmly, then looked him directly in the eye. "In fact, it couldn't be better." She started to giggle when she saw Brandon gesturing wildly from the doorway. "I'll have to get back to you on *Running Scared*. I promise, I'll be in touch."

Jeff's puzzled expression made her start to laugh openly. "I'm really sorry about this, but I have to go!" She slipped past him and darted toward the doorway. Behind her Andrea could hear Jennifer chuckling, telling Jeff to sit down.

As soon as she reached the doorway, Brandon grabbed her arm and pulled her out onto the dark, quiet street. "I've been wanting to do this for years," he whispered as he wrapped his arms around her.

Andrea held him close, his heart beating in her ear. "Me too, Brandon, me too!" she confided as she stretched up to meet his waiting lips.

"Andrea Zuckerman, I didn't know you had it in you!" Kelly teased, her eyes wide with mock indignation.

"So who was he?" Donna asked as she stood up and shook the sand off her legs.

Andrea looked up at her in confusion. "Who was who?"

"Your mystery man! Who else?" Donna stamped her foot impatiently.

"He was just this guy," Andrea stammered as she saw Brenda and Kelly start to giggle. When she had told her fantasy out loud, Andrea hadn't named Brandon. Now she had to worm her way out of this without giving it away.

"What'd he look like?" Brenda asked pointedly.

"I told you, Brenda. Really, you guys are starting to get on my nerves." Andrea bent over to pick up the discarded bags of munchies that lay around the dying fire.

"Kind of sensitive, aren't you, Andrea?" Dylan eyed her coolly and Andrea felt her face flush.

"Well, you know, after you tell your deepest secrets, it's kind of weird to have to rehash every detail with your friends," Andrea said defensively.

"All I asked was what he looked like," Brenda restated.

"Yeah, Andrea, what's the big deal?" Brandon turned to her with a frown. "It's not like any of us are going to say anything."

There was no way out. Even David Silver sat waiting for her answer. Andrea took a deep breath and gazed across at Brenda, venom dripping in her eyes. "I guess you could say he's kind of cute, in a wholesome

way. Uh, he's got wavy, light brown hair, really blue eyes, and a nice smile. Nothing too spectacular."

Kelly nudged Brenda and smirked. "Sounds like someone we know, Andrea."

"No, I don't think so, Kelly. See"—her mind raced to fill in the words—"I made him up as I went along. You know, a piece here, another piece there."

"So you're saying he's a figment of your imagination," Brenda said in a doubtful tone.

"Right, exactly." Andrea tossed the bags next to her blanket and stood with her arms folded.

"Right . . ." Donna said as she raised her eyebrows in disbelief at Andrea.

"I'm telling you, I made him up." Her voice grew tense as she felt Dylan and Brandon staring at her.

"Fine," Brenda answered dryly. "It's just that the guy you described sounds like someone we all know, that's all. No need to get all upset."

Andrea glared at Brenda, then sat back down, her eyes locked on the fire.

"Who does it sound like, Bren?" Brandon asked in a hoarse whisper.

Brenda looked at her brother in surprise then shook her head with a smile. Dylan caught her eye and made a flying motion above Brandon's head. He still didn't get it, even after that, she thought. Brenda glanced over at Andrea, sitting with her back razor straight underneath the gold sweatshirt. "No one you know, Brandon," she said softly.

Kelly smiled and nodded her head approvingly as Andrea smiled gratefully at Brenda. Brandon sat silently with a confused expression on his face, trying to put together the pieces.

If Brandon couldn't figure it out by himself, Brenda thought, then he didn't deserve to know. With a wink at Andrea, Brenda wrapped her arms around Dylan and they tumbled onto the sand laughing.

Epilogue

THE OCEAN BREEZE GREW STEADY AND THE low flames flared in the sudden wind, the red-hot coals bright as the night air whisked over them. "I'm getting cold," Kelly whined, and pulled her blanket tight around her.

"Yeah, I think it's time we call it a night. What do you say, Minnesota?" Dylan slapped Brandon on the shoulder.

"Huh, what?" Brandon looked dazedly around the fire. "What'd you say?"

"Dylan said maybe it's time to pack it in," Steve explained with a chuckle. "Where's your head at?"

"I was just trying to figure out who the guy was in Andrea's fantasy," he answered. He didn't want to admit it, but it was really eating at him for some reason. "He'd have to be one tough cookie to break

through her armor." Brandon laughed as Andrea stuck her tongue out at him.

"C'mon, Hobson, drop it! The lady said she made it up, then she made it up, dig?" Dylan gestured toward Andrea. "Besides, this was supposed to be all in good fun, remember?"

"Yeah, and it was a lot of fun, too," Brenda added with a grin. "So what do you guys say we make a promise right here that no matter where we go or what we do, ten years from now we get together for a reunion and compare our real lives to our fantasies." She squatted on her knees, looking for reactions around the circle.

"Sounds cool to me," Kelly answered.

"Me too! But isn't ten years too long a time?" Donna said as she piled up the empty soda cans.

"Donna, that's how long from now it was supposed to be in our fantasies, remember?" David shook his head then leaned over to toss a can in the cooler.

"Oh, yeah, that's right," Donna smiled meekly back at him.

"Hey, wait a minute here. How do I know if I'll be anywhere around here in ten years? What am I supposed to do, drop everything and come running for a stupid reunion to compare our fantasies? No way! I didn't want to do this in the beginning and I definitely don't want to do it ten years." Steve shook his head firmly.

"Fine, Steve, you don't have to come. We all know that there's no way that your real life could come close to what you described in your fantasy anyway." Kelly's face was expressionless.

"Very cute," Steve snapped as he moved toward her.

"C'mon, you two, would you knock it off!" Andrea placed her hand against Steve's chest, pushing him backward.

"Brenda, don't you think that making promises

about the future is too risky?" David spoke with earnestness.

"Why would I think that?" Brenda asked sarcastically.

"Well, what if something happens to you along the way, and then you have to come back here and listen to what everyone else accomplished. It could be really depressing," David explained.

"I'm not worried about it, David, I'm sure that my life will be similar to what I told you guys." Brenda ran her fingers through Dylan's hair.

"Must be nice," Andrea muttered under her breath.

"What'd you say?" Brandon asked her as he held the opposite end of the blanket they were folding.

"Uh, nothing. Never mind, Brandon." Andrea held her end up as he walked toward her.

"C'mon, you guys, let's promise. Hold your hands out," Brenda instructed, holding her own just above the coals. "Everyone hold on to the person's hand next to you. Right."

They all moved in closer and formed a tight circle. "Now what, Bren?" Dylan glanced at his girlfriend for instructions.

"I don't know, I guess we should all repeat something like 'No matter where I am or whom I'm with, in ten years I promise to come back to the beach for a reunion.' How's that?"

"Kind of long," Steve mumbled, then stopped when Kelly kicked his shin lightly.

"It sounds perfect," Donna answered firmly.

"It does, Bren," Kelly agreed.

"So are you going to lead us?" Andrea kept her eyes away from Brandon's face.

"Sure, okay, everyone repeat after me." Brenda bowed her head and spoke quietly. "No matter where we are . . ."

"No matter where we are . . ."

"No matter who we're with . . ." she continued.

"No matter who I'm with . . ." Steve grinned suggestively at Kelly.

"In ten years' time we promise to come back to the beach for a reunion," Brenda finished.

"In ten years' time we promise to come back to the beach for a reunion," everyone repeated.

"Great!" Brenda exclaimed, and leaned over to pick up her blanket.

"I don't know what's so great about it, Bren. Big deal! We say we're going to do this, but who knows where we'll all be in ten years. Anything can happen," Brandon complained.

"Why don't you put a clamp on it, Brandon," Brenda suggested with a smirk.

Brandon frowned at his sister. "You know, when I first got here tonight, I tried to tell you guys what it felt like having someone bossing me around all summer. So what happens? Now my sister has managed to make plans for me—in ten years!" He kicked his sneaker deep into the sand, covering the coals and killing the fire.

"Oh, Brandon, you always have to have something to whine about," Brenda said as she tucked the blanket under her arm.

"Come on, Hobson, what do you say we let it rest, okay?" Dylan said as he put his arm around Brandon's shoulder.

"But, D., man, listen to what I'm saying. Someone's always telling me what to do," Brandon continued as they started to make their way up the beach.

"Yeah, yeah. It's a tough life, isn't it?" Dylan answered as everyone laughed and set out into the darkness, the silence of the summer night settling behind them.

Go back to the beginning...
See the 90 minutes that started it all!

THE BEVERLY HILLS, 90210 HOME VIDEO
available in video stores everywhere January 1992.

Don't Miss An Issue!